The Bend In The Tracks

Christopher Barry

DEDICATION

For my son,

And all my friends who helped me along the way

CONTENTS

The Bend In The Tracks

CHAPTER 1

Tom Dickens walked out of his house into the cool early morning air, quickly closing the front door behind him as he stepped off the porch. He looked to the skies and gripped his coffee. He was pleased to see that the visibility was manageable, some clouds and light fog would not stop him today. Tom rubbed his beard and let out a tired yawn, shaking his head to try and fully wake up. The aroma of the black coffee poured over him. His mind was at ease knowing it would do the trick in no time at all. He reached his blue truck in the driveway and gently opened the door, careful not to move too suddenly in order to save his coffee from being spilled. He set the coffee in the cup holder and climbed onto the single bench seat in his old truck, turned the key, and started down his long dirt driveway. Tom had lived in the country all his life so it was only natural for him to have a farm of his own and continue doing what he loved. He was a farmer by nature, but had another passion that he had taken up as a full-time career. His office was only a few miles away, a ten-minute drive for a morning like this.

He gazed out at the fields and open lands as he drove past. The morning dew that clung to the barbed wire fences lining the road, glistened in the sunshine of the new day. He smiled as he picked up his mug to take a sip. The radio DJ cut in after a commercial break announcing that it was going to be another hot day in the Fresno and

Madera area. The DJ faded out as Jack Johnson faded into the truck's speakers, filling the cab with a sweet melody.

The truck carefully pulled into the parking space in front of the office. The lyrics were stuck in his head as he turned off the truck and climbed out. He started to shut the door when he realized he nearly forgot his coffee. He reached back in and grabbed it with precision, as if to never let it out of his sight again. He walked to the office door that had his name across the glass window and a picture of an airplane. Tom knew exactly how to jingle the lock in order to get the door to open on the first try; he had done so, thousands of times. The lights in the office sprang on as he flipped the switch.

It was a small office, slightly larger than the average bedroom, but that was not where he mainly worked. The office was used to keep records, run his business, and meet new clients. The real work took place through the next door. Tom shuffled across the room, unlatched the back door and walked into a dark airplane hangar. The fluorescent lights buzzed as they all came on in order. There in front of Tom sat an old '76 Grumman Ag Cat. It was a beautiful old bi plane that had originally been a dull yellow color. Tom Dickens had gotten tired of that color so he painted it a bright red so it would really stand out. He opened the giant hangar doors and pulled the airplane out to prepare it for its flight.

Hersey the cat wandered over to see what all the commotion was. He was a black and grey cat that Tom had gotten a few years before in order to keep the rodent problem down around his office. Hersey had done his job well because now he was big and sluggish as he waddled towards the plane. He carefully jumped onto the tail of the airplane and sat down next to the coffee mug that had been placed there just moments before. He curled into a ball to lie down and relax after his strenuous activity.

Hersey watched as Tom did his last preflight checks before climbing into the cockpit to warm up the engine. When Tom climbed down he shooed Hersey away so that he would not get hurt once the airplane started moving. Tom took his last sips of his coffee, trying to savor every last drop before walking the mug back to the safety of his office. He was filled with excitement as he walked back to the plane. After years of flying he had never gotten tired of it. He glanced at a small sticker he had gotten from his wife years ago for his birthday that read, 'Man made planes to fly with the Angels'. With a big grin from ear to ear, he climbed in and started moving towards the runway.

With a deep breath and a moment of clarity, he pushed the engine to full throttle and the airplane screamed down the runway. The plane shook as it gained speed until finally the wheels left the ground and he climbed into the sky. Tom felt relaxed as he looked down at the ground passing quickly below him. He had a few fields to work on today, so it would only take a couple of hours, yet he knew he would enjoy every minute of it.

Tom quickly spotted the stream he knew he had to follow to get to the first field. He dipped, dived and rolled through the clouds, mimicking the freedom of a bird. He saw the train tracks below and knew he had reached his destination. He dropped down close to the ground, swooping across the tracks as the train rolled by underneath him. He flipped the switch to dust the crops for his first pass and flew out over the field unaware of the people that may be on the train below, slowly making their way through the farmland.

CHAPTER 2

A young man sat comfortably in his seat on the train. He stared out the window watching the grassy farmland roll by. Music seeped through his headphones as he listened to "Breakdown" by Jack Johnson. His mind was fixed on the night ahead. The train creaked and squeaked as it rounded a soft bend in the tracks. His sunglasses were pulled tight for fear of a stray beam of light penetrating his innocent eyes. He could still feel the party from the night before as his body ached. Since he had been staring out the window almost the entire ride, it would seem that he should be seated closest to the window. Nevertheless, his precious guitar held the prize position as he glanced over it from the aisle seat, watching the sunrise above the horizon. He did not mind at all though, that guitar was his life. Someone had once told him if he treated it right, he would never have to work a day in his life. In his world that guitar was royalty and things had been working out quite nicely.

From his seat, he had a perfect view down the aisle of the train. There were not too many passengers, maybe because it was 8 o'clock in the morning on a Saturday. No businessmen today, just weary travelers moving about in different times of their lives. He could see an older woman in the row in front of him sitting on the opposite side of the train. She had a book in hand that had not moved the entire trip, except for the occasional page flipping here and there. He assumed she must be a grandmother by the way she focused on her book. Probably a love story or maybe a murder mystery, something an old person would like. Or it could be that he gathered this information from the tag clinging to the top of her luggage reading 'World's Greatest Grandma' sitting down by her feet. He glanced further down the aisle, curious as to who else could be along for the ride. Two rows ahead sat a man in his early thirties, he assumed. The only thing truly visible was a skull and flames tattoo on his left forearm as it hung from the armrest. But what really caught his eye was the girl sitting four rows ahead. She had yet to turn around so all he could see so far was her beautiful dark brown hair. She sat in the row across from him and kept turning to the seat next to her.

She must be talking to a friend, he thought. Maybe she's single? What if she's not? She's probably sitting next to her boyfriend. She's probably ugly anyway.

She suddenly stood up to reveal the profile of a beautiful young woman. He was instantly mesmerized as she stood there before him, like a goddess. An unknown source passed light through the windows as if a spotlight was focused on her, as she stood on display. She slowly made her way down the aisle right towards him. He could hardly contain his sheer amazement as she neared. His thoughts almost exploded out of his head.

What can I say? I have to find out her name. I have to know all about her. Things like, what she likes to do? Is she creative? Does she draw, swim, or hike? Can she surf? Does she smile a lot? Can she dance? Does she make funny noises when she laughs too hard? Does she curl her toes when she orgasms? I just have to know.

She suddenly passed without a word being said. He thought to himself that he had lost his chance, as he gazed back out the window and tried to count the cows as they passed. Still thinking of the girl, he believed the excitement got the best of him. He thought that if he had played it cool, it would have been fine. Suddenly she came walking back. She must have been going to buy a drink or something because she asked her friend for some more money, he thought to himself. A blonde haired girl revealed herself from her seat. Relief, it's not her boyfriend. He thought she was pretty, but not the same as the other. She handed her friend two dollars out of her purse as they laughed and giggled at one another. The girl turned around and started back down the aisle straight towards him. He did not expect this; he was not prepared. If only he had something to say to her. She was two steps away from walking past him and out of his life forever.

"Excuse me miss, do you know which station is next? I'm not too familiar with this train," he bellowed out. Feeling like an idiot, he was sure she would just pass him off as any other random encounter.

"I think the next stop is Merced. I'm not really sure. This is my second time taking this train," she replied as she slowed down to take a better look at this stranger. She was intrigued by this man and did not know why. She found herself standing in front of a young man with long blonde hair and mirrored sunglasses. The holes in his Nirvana shirt and dark blue jeans match perfectly as if he had carved them out on the same day. A flannel jacket flowed effortlessly over his shoulders and down his body. She stood there amazed, almost as if maybe she had seen him before somewhere. "Is this your first time on the train?" she asked.

"Yeah," he answered quickly, knowing full well that he had been on the train many times before. He now saw he had a real chance to talk to her. He wanted to say something witty, but nothing came to mind. "I'm headed home to Stockton for the Memorial Day weekend. Where are you off to?" He hoped that he could just keep the conversation going for even another minute.

"I live in Tracy, but my friend is going to drive us from Stockton. It's where we left from," she answered in a sweet voice, almost too beautiful to be real.

"That's cool. Where are you coming from?" he asked, seeming very interested, yet trying to play it cool. He knew he now had the fish ready to take the bait, but would she bite at the risk being pulled in?

"We went down to visit some friends for the week in Bakersfield. We would have stayed all weekend, but my friend has some stuff going on today back home."

"Bet that was fun! That means you've been on the train for quite awhile now," he said with more of a statement than a question.

"Yeah," she let out a breath as if she was tired of being on the train. She glances over to see the guitar. Pointing at it she asked, "Do you play?"

Noticing her attempt to keep the conversation going he replied excitedly, "Yes, just a little."

"I would love to hear it sometime," she smiled as she said it. "Are you in a band or anything?" she asked.

"Kinda," he said as if it is no big deal. "We mostly mess around, jam and have fun. Do you play?" he added. He had always found girl musicians fascinating, but they were hard to come by.

"I tried a few times, but it was way too hard and hurts my fingers too much," she said with a sad tone as she glanced at her fingers as if to prove the point further. She slowly shifted her weight from one leg to the other as if she was getting tired of standing.

Noticing the movement he asked, "Would you like to sit down?" gesturing to the seat clearly taken by the guitar.

She smiled then said, "I would love to, but I'm supposed to be getting a soda for me and my friend." She thought for a second then added, "But afterwards if she doesn't mind I could come back or something?" She had a nervous, but hopeful look on her face as she gently bit her lower lip.

"I would love that!" he answered immediately.

"My name is Lila by the way," she added.

He said his name and they exchanged smiles before she wandered off down the hall. He looked at his phone to check the time. He knew there was still an hour and a half until he would be home. Plenty of time to get to know this girl, or really mess it up in that case. He quickly flipped through his music on his phone finally settling on Social Distortion, "Story of my Life". He knew she would be back in a few minutes, but this time he was not too nervous. There was something calming about talking to her. Something in her voice that seemed magical. He gazed out the window once more, still thinking about the night ahead. His fingers started to move with excitement. He could imagine how it was going to be.

Just then, Lila walked by with two ice-cold sodas in her hands. She gave a heartwarming smile as she passed. He watched her walk down the aisle to her seat. Her hips swayed in perfect elegance from side to side in her tight jeans. Her white shirt blew in the breeze of her movement as she floated down the aisle. Arriving at her seat, she handed a soda over to her friend. He could only imagine what they could possibly be saying to one another. He fantasized how the friend was asking why it took so long. She was probably telling her all about how she talked to some guy on the way and he seemed really nice.

Lila leaned in close and whispered something in her friend's ear. He played with his phone as if to not be analyzing every movement she made with absolute awe. Her friend leaned out over the seats into the aisle and stared straight at him with a smile. She then pulled Lila close to her and whispered something back. In a sweeping motion she shoved Lila down the aisle towards him. Lila instantly turned red with embarrassment as her friend laughed and told her aloud to go sit next to him. He laughed a little at the site he just witnessed and set his phone back on his lap.

She walked to him with her arms crossed behind her back as if to be an innocent little schoolgirl and asked politely, "Can I sit with you?" She was nervous, even though she already knew his answer.

He said yes as he moved the guitar to the seat across the aisle. He then moved to the seat closest to the window as he offered her a place to sit.

"Isn't the country lovely?" she asked as she stared out the window.

"I love the country," he replied. "If I could, I would have a house out in the country with tons of land."

She turned to him as her face lit up. "That would be my dream! I've always wanted to have a bunch of cows and a horse…"

"And chickens!" he added jokingly.

"And tons of chickens!" she said excitedly. "And it can have a cute little barn to go along with the pink farmhouse," Lila added with a playful grin.

He laughed as he asked, "Does the farmhouse have to be pink? Why not white?"

Acting as if she was shocked at his question, "Of course it has to be pink or else it won't match the purple barn!"

They slowly grew very comfortable with one another the more they talked.

"What type of things do you like to do?" he asked.

She thought for a second, "I don't know, like what?"

"Well" he replied, "Do you draw, sing, dance, swim, hike, surf, do you make funny noises when you laugh?" For some reason he forgot to ask about the curling of the toes.

This made her laugh. "Well, I don't think I make funny noises when I laugh."

She went on to tell him a little bit about herself. She was born in Santa Cruz and lived there until she was three. Her father had gotten a promotion at his job, but could only have it if they moved. Her mother was an interior designer so she had no problem picking up and leaving for her husband, but they did miss the beach quite a bit, and they did not expect the heat that came with moving to the valley. For as long as she could remember, they have gone back to Santa Cruz every few months to visit her cousins and her grandparents on her mother's side. Her father's parents lived in Santa Barbara so she only gets to visit them once or twice a year. She had gone to two different elementary schools because of an overflow of students in her district. The second school went all the way through middle school, so she went straight to high school after. Instead of going to a university, she stayed close to home and attended a community college.

She told him all about her favorite places to go by the ocean and they both realized they had a lot in common. He had frequented Santa Cruz quite a bit throughout his life as well. She told stories of her childhood, shared funny holiday moments, and even about the time where she knocked over her own birthday cake onto herself.

He countered with how he could ride his bike with no hands at the age of six, would build zip lines from his tree house with his friends, and how when he was thirteen he learned how to drive a car, which happened to be a stick shift, in a field, while his cousin fed their grandmother's cattle.

As time went on they tried to one up one another with the silliest and craziest stories they could possibly think of. He had never met someone in which he felt so comfortable with, in so little time. It amazed him as he thought about it. He wanted to know anything and everything about this girl. He wanted to let her into his life. As if to open up his memories and let her watch them like old movies from a projector.

She pulled her face closer to his and carefully took off his glasses.

"Where did you get these?" she asked.

He was quick to reply with a smart remark, "Down in Paraguay last summer." He tried to hold back the laughter with a simple smile, finally losing the battle when he simply found his statement too silly.

Suspicious by his laugh she questioned him, "Did you really go to Paraguay?" Even though she was sure he had not.

"No," he replied, giving in so easily to his gag. "I got them at a gas station about a year ago."

Playing with the glasses in her hands she looked into his eyes realizing that this was the first time she had seen them. She took in the remarkable shade of blue that was set before her, leaving her utterly speechless for a moment. She had been wondering what they looked like, but she had not expected this.

Bumbling down the aisle, Lila's friend came walking up to them.

"I'm bored," she announced. "You left me all alone for like an hour!"

He had not realized that an hour had already gone by. That meant that there was only another thirty minutes or so until they reached their destination. He wondered what would happen then, if he would ever see her again.

"So what have you guys been talking about for so long?" she asked.

Lila thought for a second then replied, "Oh you know, the normal random stuff." Leaning in to him she added, "By the way, this is my friend Stacy."

Lila went on to introduce her new friend and tell Stacy a little about what she had learned of him. She recapped some of the funny stories as the three of them laughed and contributed their little jokes and input into the stories. Stacy was a little blonde woman with a bubbly personality. She had her moments with ditzy comments and silly actions in which everyone passed off as being blonde. She was very nice though, one of those friends you could really count on for anything and always loved to have a good time.

Stacy admired Lila's new find and was interested in this new person. She asked questions of her own to try and piece together the mystery in front of her.

"So what do you do down in Fresno?" she wondered.

He replied quickly, "Well, I go to Fresno State, but I come back home all the time to visit because my friends and family live in Stockton."

Intrigued with his answer she added, "Very cool, how do you like it there?" She had not gone away to college after high school, instead she stayed at home and went to the community college nearby.

He was reluctant to answer this question because there was more to the story then he really wanted to say, "It's alright, it's just not the same as being home." He hated Fresno and wished that he could be anywhere else.

Not quite sensing the hesitation, she continued to press him for answers. "How are the people? Have you made a lot of friends?"

"Oh yes." he replied. "The people are amazing, and the parties are even better. We had this huge party last night that was a ton of fun! My friends got me to stand on this counter top at some girl's place and sing all these random songs to everyone as they recorded it. How embarrassing!" He became excited as he remembered the previous night.

Lila, impressed with the story said, "That sounds like fun! Can you sing?"

"Hardly," he joked. "That's what makes it even worse!"

Stacy found humor in the story and added, "I would have loved to see that!" She giggled as she tried to imagine the event taking place.

"I bet you sound fine," Lila stated with a smile.

He turned to her and they locked eyes once again. Suddenly he felt as if the world around them had fallen away and nothing else mattered, but her.

"Maybe I'll sing for you sometime," he said in a low loving voice.

"I would love that," she replied as she slowly bit her lower lip. Her eyes were gazing back and forth over his lips as if she was anticipating a kiss about to come. Her left hand had come to rest on his knee while her right hand gently touched his arm, caressing her fingers in small patterns along it.

"I wish I could sing," interrupted Stacy as she shattered the moment. "That would be so cool, I would sing all the time," Stacy rambled on; mainly to herself because she was unaware that no one there was paying attention to her. She had a history of doing this a lot and it never seemed to bother her, probably because she had never noticed that it was happening.

Lila had started to wonder what was going to happen as they neared the station. She knew that in not too long she would have to leave and she was unsure when she would get the chance to see him again. She could not remember the last time someone had made her feel this way, if ever. Unable to completely describe the feelings she had towards this person, she knew she only wanted more. If only there was some way to spend more time with him. She thought about how she could come visit him while he was home for the weekend, or possibly go down to Fresno to stay with him. Maybe he would like to come visit her sometime. But what was she thinking; this was someone she had met just an hour earlier. How could she be thinking this far ahead already? Little did she know, he had been thinking the same thing the entire time.

"Next stop Stockton," the intercom blared. "Arrival time, ten minutes."

Time had been going by so fast this morning he thought. He was grateful to have met such a beautiful young woman along the way. Without her, it would have been a long trip. Stacy realized that her and Lila's bags had been left on the seats they had abandoned some time ago.

"I'll go grab our stuff!" she exclaimed as she got up from her seat and made her way down the aisle.

They both knew what was coming next and they did not want it to end with a simple hug on a train platform.

"Would you and Stacy like to have breakfast with me before you two leave town?" he asked eagerly. He was hoping that she would take any reason to stay longer with him.

She thought about the offer for a second then replied, "I would love too, but Stacy has to be back home by ten because she has to go to her grandmother's birthday lunch with her family." She seemed sad as she turned the offer down.

Stacy carried the bags back down the aisle and plopped them down in front of her new seat. Over hearing the question she added, "Lila, you can go if you want, that is if he is willing to take you home after."

Ecstatic, Lila turned to him and asked, "Would that be alright with you?" She sat hopeless for an answer.

He was so excited he could barely get the words out, "Of course, I have no problem with that."

In her excitement, she could not help but lean over and give him a kiss on the cheek. He thought that this must be too good to be true because opportunities like this very rarely present themselves in real life.

Stacy finally stated what was on everyone's mind, "That'll be perfect because then you two can spend more time together."

"Are you sure you'll be okay without me?" Lila asked to double check.

"Of course girl, I'll be fine," she said as she pulled a piece of gum out of her pocket to chomp on. "Call me when you're done with breakfast, okay?"

The train slowly came to a stop in the station. Stacy snatched her bags and headed for the door. Lila gracefully stood up and grabbed her belongings as he carefully picked up his guitar. Cradling it in his arms he asked if it missed him. This made Lila laugh and smile at this person who seemed so innocent with his guitar. He gently placed his hand on her lower back as they made their way to the exit of the train. Stepping outside, the sun was intensely bright as he found his glasses in which Lila had placed hanging from his jacket chest pocket. He steadily placed them back over his eyes, careful to protect them from the beady rays of the sun. He glanced around his surroundings as if entering a new world for the first time.

They slowly made their way to the parking lot. Luckily, they had not parked very far from each other. They stopped at Stacy's car to say their goodbyes and helped her load her bags into the front seat of a newer model Toyota. Stacy promised to text Lila once she got home so they knew she had made the trip safely. Stacy told them to have a nice breakfast as she started the car and inched her way out of the parking spot careful not to hit the big white truck clearly parking over the lines leaving her with only inches to squeeze by. Cursing and excitement came flying through the windows as she made it through the last bit of the gauntlet and slowly started to pull out of the parking lot.

He led her to the front of an old car. She did not see it, not so much as old, but a classic.

"This is your car?" she asked curiously.

Grinning ear to ear he replied, "Yes. This is my baby."

They stood before a 1966 silver blue metallic Mustang. The body was not too bad. A few blemishes here and there, but what do you expect for a car so old, he thought to himself. The bumper drooped down slightly to the left side, but someone could only tell if they stared at it for a long time. The interior had seen better days. It had sunspots and a few tears in the seats, but they had never been replaced because the car was completely original.

"So do your parents let you borrow it every once in a while?" asked Lila, not completely clear on the situation. She stood next to him with both of her hands clenching her luggage as she stared up into his big blue eyes. She had not realized until now how tall he had been. He was an easy six feet tall while she was an average five foot, six inches.

Shocked at the question he answered, "No it's mine, I take it everywhere."

"That's awesome!" she added.

He moved to the trunk to put the guitar in and made room next to the spare tire and miscellaneous tools that clearly had a tool box hiding in the corner, but were never properly put away. She placed her bags on top of the guitar as if the trunk was too dirty to have her stuff in. He had to slam the trunk closed to get it to latch properly. Satisfied with his efforts, he made his way to the driver door.

"Hop in," he told her as he got inside the car.

She grabbed the handle half expecting it not to open because he had not unlocked the doors yet, so it surprised her when the door effortlessly opened in her hand.

Extremely surprised she said, "You mean to tell me that you left your car here and didn't even lock it?"

She still had the surprised look on her face as she climbed in the car.

"Yeah," he answered quickly. "The doors can't lock because the locks broke a few months ago, so I always keep it unlocked." He always found it funny because no one else in their right mind would ever leave a door unlocked, let alone a whole car.

15

Curious she asked, "So since you leave it unlocked all the time, does anyone ever mess with it?"

"Oh yeah," he said, nodding his head in agreement. "A few months ago my radio quit working so I had to drive everywhere in silence. It was torture! Then someone broke in one night and tried to steal my stereo, but since it is in the dash they couldn't pull it out so they tried pushing it in and ended up fixing it perfectly," he finished with a smile on his face.

He turned the key and the car let out a roar as the engine fired up. The radio came blaring on almost ear piercing loud over the engine. He carefully reached his arm under the dash to pull the stereo forward, which caused static to take over the radio. Then, with his other hand, he turned the volume down to a reasonable level and placed the stereo back into its place, turning the static into music again.

"That's a little better." He stated, with a smile.

An old country song that she had never heard before was playing as he flipped through the stations. He landed on a rock station she did not recognize. The slogan was playing and she realized that it was a Sacramento rock station. That explained why she had not heard of it, she lived too far away to get any stations from Sacramento. A song started as she thought to herself that it sounded familiar as it slowly made its way into the beat.

"It's "Garden Grove" by Sublime, have you heard it? I love this song." He was an unofficial expert on anything music. He had studied songs, bands, and genres throughout his life.

The excitement filled the air. "I love this song! But really, who doesn't love Sublime?" Lila quickly replied.

This made him happy. The biggest turn on for him was a girl who loved and appreciated music. He had spent many hours debating, defending, and appreciating the beautiful music Sublime had to offer.

Just as Lila realized the mustang was a stick shift, he jammed the car into first gear and they took off out of the parking lot. Lila reminded him of a girl he once knew by the way she sat in the passenger seat. She was almost turned completely sideways in the seat to face him as he drove with her knees so close to the stick shift that his hands brushed her legs as he reached third gear. When this happened he smiled at her before returning his eyes to the road.

"Do you like Mexican food?" he asked as the car slowed down at a stop sign. He could tell the car was a little cold because it was having trouble getting in and out of second gear. Usually with a car this old, most people would let it warm up before driving somewhere, but he never did. He did not have time for that, he was always on the go and could not wait for something pointless like that. "I know a place not too far from here that has really good breakfast burritos," he added.

"That sounds good!" she yelled, trying to be louder than the radio and noises of the car.

"Perfect!" he replied as he started singing along with the song. It was nearing his favorite part and he hated when he missed it. "Finding roaches in the POT! Wow, all these things I do, they're waiting for you. . ." he exclaimed with extra emphasis on the word pot. It was a tradition so to speak, that had been started a long time ago with his friends. It was the only line in the song that truly puzzled them. It could either stand for finding roaches, as it being the end of a joint, in a jar used to store them until enough were collected to finally smoke; or, finding cockroaches in the weed stash. Maybe, simply, it was finding roaches in the pot. Whichever way it was, it was truly a mystery to him, so once out of sheer frustration, he screamed the word pot and it had stuck ever since.

She had been trying to figure him out the entire time. Everything about him was so unique that she could not help but keep watching for what was coming next. Even down to the simplest of gestures. The way he would pretend to play drums on the steering wheel as he drove, mimicking the notes perfectly with no effort at all and gently singing along as if he had practiced every part of the song over and over until perfected.

He turned and smiled at her not realizing that she was studying him and quickly looked back towards the road. As he came to the stop sign, she watched as he effortlessly held down the clutch with his left foot while pumping the brakes with his right foot, all the while never missing a moment of the song.

It was midmorning and the sun was slowly warming the day. It had been forecasted to be low 90's and clear. The car had heated up quite a bit sitting in the parking lot. He started off from the stop sign, systematically making his way through the gears and back up to speed. Lila had noticed some very unique knobs in the center of the dashboard underneath the radio. They were little silver knobs attached to levers that fed into the dash.

"If you want your window down just tell me and I'll help you," he said as he moved the knobs in sequence to cause the cool morning air to shoot through the vents.

"Is the window broken?" she seemed puzzled at the suggestion.

Reaching across her, he smacked the glove compartment causing it to fall open, "Not necessarily," he stated still with a warm smile on his face as he pulled out a window lever and handed it to her.

Lila giggled as she realized that it had not been on the door. She took the lever from his hand and slowly placed it on a bare piece of metal protruding from the door. The lever did not slide as easy as she had expected.

Noticing that she was having trouble, he offered some advice, "Just smack it."

She made her hand into a fist and tapped the lever into place. From there she was able to turn it with ease as the window came down.

"That's interesting," she said as she laughed. She was already amazed by what she had experienced with this person and the day had just begun.

The streets were coming alive with people and cars busily rushing about their day. The sunlight glistened from the big windows on the buildings looking down at the city. Lila had never been here before. This was not really a big city, but she thought it seemed nice.

They rounded a corner as he pointed out a small restaurant in the middle of a sea of businesses. "That's where we're going," he told her. They pulled into a parking lot on the backside of the building. There were a few cars, but nothing close to filling up the parking lot; it was too early for that. The car came to rest in a parking spot not far from the front door.

He was excited as he turned off the engine. She was almost sad to have his driving come to an end. He had conducted the car as if it were his own personal orchestra.

"Are you ready to eat?" he asked as he unbuckled the lap belt.

"Of course! I'm starving, I haven't eaten yet today," Lila replied as she unbuckled her seatbelt and began to climb out of the car. He met her in front of the car and they walked to the door together. Quickly grabbing the door, he opened it as Lila slid inside.

CHAPTER 3

The restaurant was known for its authentic Mexican food. It had been one of his favorite restaurants all of his life. The inside was decorated with all types of pictures and items hanging on the wall that had Mexican heritage as music slowly seeped in to fill the background. A chalk sign greeted them that read, "Please Seat Yourself." He took her hand and guided her to a small table for two along the wall.

"This is one of my favorite places," he explained as they sat down. He had been here so many times that he did not need a menu. He rarely strayed far from what he had always ordered. She picked up the menu from her place setting and started thumbing through.

"What do you usually have?" she asked as she read the specials.

"I usually get a chicken quesadilla lunch special, but the breakfast burritos are good too," he said trying to help out.

She pondered for a moment before replying, "It all sounds really good, I don't know what to have yet."

"I'm sure whatever you decide will be perfect," he added with a smile.

She liked it when he smiled. He had a big smile that could brighten up a room with ease. It could make the saddest person happy even for a moment.

"Tell me something else about yourself, I want to know

everything," he said without hesitation.

She thought for a moment about the topics they had already covered. "I do have one hobby, I like to take pictures," she was nervous as she said it because not very many people knew this about her.

His face lit up as he said, "That's so cool! What do you take pictures of?"

"Anything really, mostly friends and family, trees, plants, whatever I find that looks interesting," she stated as she giggled. "Sometimes I go to the park and take pictures of strangers as they are walking around or sitting and relaxing. I like to capture them doing everyday things. That's my favorite."

Before she could continue a waitress appeared to take their orders, "How are you doing today?"

"Doing great, it looks like it's going to be a nice day today," he added with a smile.

Pulling out her pad of paper and a pencil, the waitress replied, "Yes it does, it should be a very nice day today. What can I get for you two?"

"I'll have the chicken quesadilla lunch special please," he asked.

"Ok, and for you sweetie?" the waitress asked Lila.

"May I have the same thing?" she replied.

"Of course dear," she said with a smile. "Anything to drink?"

"Water is fine with me," he added.

"Water sounds great," Lila stated as she closed the menu and handed it to the waitress.

The waitress smiled and walked back towards the kitchen.

"What were we talking about a moment ago?" Lila asked as she tried to recall the conversation.

"I think you were talking about how you are a creeper and stalk people in the park with a camera," he said with a laugh.

"I am not a creeper!" she tried to say in her defense. "I just like to capture the moment when it's real."

She knew he was playing around, but she still shot him eye darts followed by a smile to let him know it was all right. While they teased each other, she started to think about what they were going to do for the rest of the day. She was sure by now that they would spend most of the day together. There was no way she was about to go home after breakfast. Besides, she had no other plans for the day.

"What should we do today?" she asked, curious as to what his answer could be.

He was excited to hear this question because he had been trying to plan out their day together the entire time. "I'm glad you asked, I have an idea for after we eat," he said as the waitress appeared with their food.

She slid the hot plates on the table grateful to get them off her burning fingers. "Here you go," she said with a sigh of relief.

"Thank you very much," he said as he looked over his food as if it were a prize held before him.

Lila grabbed her fork and started eating in the elegant little way he had assumed she would.

"It works a lot better if you eat it like this," picking the quesadilla from the plate and demonstrating how he could eat it with his hands.

She laughed at him because she realized that he had probably never used a fork while eating a quesadilla, and her assumptions were correct. Even though he was a slob eating with his hands and dripping grease making a mess all over, she found him to be very cute in his playful childlike ways.

"So what's your idea for today?" she questioned him as he stuffed his face with cheese and chicken.

He tried to chew as quickly as possible as to not talk with his mouth full. "I was thinking that we could go to some really cool shops that are close by, they usually have a lot of random stuff to look at."

"That sounds like fun," she was interested in what kind of things they would find.

They finished their meals as the waitress brought the check to the table. "Will that be all?" she asked.

"Yes, that was perfect," he replied, as he reached for his wallet to pay the bill.

"I can pay for my half," Lila said.

With a smile he set a twenty-dollar bill on the table. "That's quite alright," he stated. "It's my treat."

The two got up from their table and made their way to the door. As he opened the door for her he noticed the rays of light had receded, as the sun grew higher into the sky. Once again, he pulled his glasses out of his jacket pocket and tightly fashioned them to his face. The step out into the cool morning air was refreshing. Lila tilted her head back as if to let as much oxygen as possible fill her lungs as she gazed at the overwhelmingly blue sky. He looked around to get his bearings; once set on a direction he grabbed her hand and they started to walk down the street. He liked the way her hands felt, so soft and feminine. He admired the way her hair whispered in the wind, the elegant and gliding movement of her body as she walked. It has to be a dream he thought, it must.

She liked the ways his hands engulfed hers. It seemed that everything about him was larger than life, she thought to herself. She focused on the way his long blonde hair moved with his body. It was so messy, yet so perfect no matter how it was. Everything about him reflected his confidence, from the way he held his body to the little smile on his face that made her feel like he knew exactly what he was doing, as if he had planned out the day before they had ever met. The only part about him that gave up any secrets was his eyes. She knew they would tell her anything if only she knew how to read them.

They rounded the corner quickly heading toward what seemed to be downtown, Lila concluded. She had not been here before so everything was new to her.

"I know some cool places around here," he told her.

Lila smiled, she would follow him anywhere.

They came upon a small antique shop. The windows were filled with clutter as they gazed inside. A man stood outside the shop with a cigarette in one hand and his coffee in the other. He greeted them with a pleasant hello as they contemplated exploring the store.

"Would you like to go inside and check it out?" he asked her, not sure if she would take any interest in the idea.

"Sounds like fun," she replied as she pulled him into the store.

The building was as cluttered as the window. Antiques were piled on top of each other as if thrown in and out of the way to make room for it all. A lamp, hats, couches, and pictures filled the doorway as they passed through. Lila found a green velvet hat with a purple feather sticking out of the top and delicately placed it on her head.

"How do I look?" she asked him sarcastically. She danced around showing off the treasure she had found, careful not to let it fall off her head as if it were made of gold.

"Stunning my dear, absolutely stunning," he said with a laugh. He admired the care she took with each step as if she had practiced a dance routine.

He grabbed a cane that was next to a box of old encyclopedias and dusted it off. It had a small piece of silver with the picture of a bird set into the handle. "How do I look?" he wondered as he posed with his find.

"You look as if you're ready for a ball, a beautifully wonderful ball, where all of the ladies gaze upon you in wonderment and can't get enough!" she enchanted.

"You're weird!" he announced as he stuck his tongue out at her.

Something caught her eye as she sifted through the room. Towards the back wall sat a glass cabinet with certain items placed inside. Lila walked over to see if she was correct in her assumption of what could be in it.

"What is it?" he asked as he walked up behind her. She stood over the glass in pure amazement as she analyzed what was inside. As he neared, he saw a small black camera inside the case. He could not tell how old it was, but he knew it was old.

She paused for a long time before finally answering, "It's a camera just like the one my grandfather once had. He would take it everywhere, it was the only one he ever used."

He stared with excitement. "Where do you get film for it?" he asked curiously.

"I'm not sure of anywhere around here. Most of the places closed down after digital cameras came out," she said in discouragement. She rubbed her fingers on the glass as if she could touch the camera.

The man smoking a cigarette had finished and walked back into the store still sipping on his coffee.

"Is there anything I can help you with?" the man asked as he rounded the counter.

"Yes, do you happen to have film for this camera by any chance?" he replied with hope in his eyes.

The man took a moment to think about the question before answering, "Sometimes we do, I can check the back real quick if you don't mind."

"No, we don't mind at all." Lila replied, jumping at the answer.

"Okay, it will be a moment," the man answered as he disappeared into the back room.

Lila's heart filled with desire. She waited patiently for the man to return with the verdict. She felt as if hours had gone by without an answer. Finally the man returned with a small box in his hands and Lila's eyes filled with hope.

"I found three rolls that will fit that camera right there in front of you," the man explained, as he pointed towards the camera.

Lila nearly jumped out of her skin with excitement. The boy she barely knew stood next to her. He had gotten lost for a moment admiring a silver watch while the man had walked back in and had almost missed the announcement.

"How much for the camera and the film?" he asked without hesitation.

The man behind the counter thought for a moment then said, "$40 for both."

"We'll take it!" he announced before Lila could chime in.

"I don't know about that," Lila added. "I don't have that much money on me and I can't ask you to buy it for me, that wouldn't be right."

He pulled $40 out of his wallet and handed it to the man behind the counter before Lila could stop him. "It would be a shame to leave such a unique camera here."

By this time Lila had become overwhelmed with excitement to the point that she could no longer protest. The man behind the counter grabbed a bag and filled it with the newly purchased items. Lila watched patiently as they were gently handled before the man handed the bag across the counter.

"I hope you two have a great day," the man said with a smile.

"I hope you do as well," Lila replied with a grin usually only reserved for a child holding a bag of candy.

The two of them walked out of the shop once again into the rays of sunlight. As if on queue, he fastened the sunglasses back onto his face with a seamless effort.

Lila presented a twenty dollar bill and handed it to him. "I can't let you pay for the whole thing," she protested.

He took the money without argument and then grabbed her soft tender hand and as her fingers locked into his he added, "There's one more place down the street that I like to go to every once in awhile."

"I would love to go!" she exclaimed with the childish smile still across her face.

He giggled as he studied her excitement over the camera still in the bag that she clenched tightly in her right hand. They started their journey down the street between the tall downtown buildings. The sun hanging high in the sky, only cast small shadows over the sidewalk now. Neither of them felt the fear of waking at any moment from this dream. This was real. That feeling of great pleasure and happiness was really there as they walked together on this still, almost unbelievable day.

As they neared the building that was to be their destination, Lila gazed at the sign hanging above reading, "Pawn Shop". In the window she could see similar items as the place before. But something did catch her attention. She noticed an old banjo and a few guitars in the window jammed within the clutter. She did not give it a second thought as they walked into the front door of the shop.

The inside of this place was different from the last. Guitars of every kind, style and color hung on the walls between the other items. Lila quickly made the connection as to why he had brought her here. A man behind the far counter of the shop greeted them as they walked in.

"Welcome! How is your day going?" said the man behind the counter.

"Very well Bill, thank you. And how is yours going?" he said in a soft peaceful tone.

"Very good as well. It has been a nice slow morning," Bill replied with a grin. "I'm glad to see you back in here. I've got something to show you," Bill added with excitement.

Bill went into the back and then quickly emerged with a white guitar in his hands and gently passed it across the counter. Lila watched as he accepted the guitar as if it were the most precious and delicate item he had ever held. He rolled it in his hands, inspecting every piece of the guitar. The name at the top read Fender as he glanced over the lettering.

"This looks like Jimi Hendrix's guitar!" he exclaimed with excitement as he twisted the price tag to reveal how much it cost.

Lila glanced over his shoulder to get a better look at the price. Noticing this he turned the tag towards her so she could read it easier. Seeing the price, her eyes widened in awe.

"And for that price it might as well have been Jimi's. I don't think I'm quite ready for that one yet," he added with a little laugh as the excitement slowly seeped out of his body.

Bill joined in with the light laughter. "No problem," he said as he reached with both hands to accept the guitar back. "I'm sure when you are ready, this one will still be waiting for you. I do have an idea of what you'll need for today."

The man with the guitar walked through the door leading to the back room of the shop. There was a small curtain that he pushed aside and let it fall back in place as he disappeared. Lila was intrigued as to what would be brought out next. She started to think back through the conversation the two men had just had. Lost in thought, she unknowingly wrapped her arm around his as they stood at the counter waiting for what would be revealed from the back room. From what he had told her on the way there, he had come here before and that was confirmed by the reaction of the man behind the counter. But there was something else, almost as an unspoken underlining communication they had.

Bill returned from the backroom, this time with a black guitar and handed it over the counter as if presenting a sword to a knight before he rode into battle. His shoulders and head even seemed to drop a little out of respect for the acceptance of this guitar. Lila found this sight more fascinating than strange.

"That's what I'm talking about!" he exclaimed in excitement. "You know me too well Bill!"

Now his smile was ear-to-ear, even bigger than the first guitar. Lila did not recognize the brand name on the neck of this guitar. She followed his hands with her eyes as he gently rolled and touched the different parts of the guitar as if his fingertips would inspect and then give him a full report later on. He caressed the neck of the guitar, slipping his fingers down it as if to caress the body of a woman. With a tenderness and elegance, he made his way down the body of the guitar and slowly touched the golden tuning knobs one by one.

"Can I try it out?" he asked almost nervously, as if there would be a chance of rejection.

"Of course you can," Bill answered, as he leaned over a table just off to his side, and picked up a guitar cable that was neatly wrapped in a tight circle. Handing it across the counter he added, "That black amp over there on the ground is plugged in, you can use that one."

Lila turned and propped her back up against the counter as she watched him walk towards the amp. As he reached it, he knelt down and began the task of setting up the guitar. Once the cord was properly plugged in and the amp was turned on he gave the guitar a quick strum. A sweet sound softly came from the amp as he worked quickly turning knobs and buttons before the sound had dissipated. He strummed once more and turned another knob until he seemed to be satisfied with himself and stood back up, ready to run his test of the guitar.

Lila watched in anticipation for the sounds to come out of the amp. She had been curious to hear him play and only now had realized this would be her first opportunity to. She gazed upon him and took note of the moment. He took a nice and smooth breath as he began to play. The amp hissed out a distorted melody as his fingers moved along the guitar. The sound of blues filled the entire shop within no time at all. She was pleased with what she heard as she began to tap her foot and bob her head to the melody. She was captivated by sound. It was smooth and elegant, yet rough and brutal all at the same time. As the sound bounced off every corner of the room, even Bill was lost in the moment as his hands started tapping to the melody.

The song had wound down just a moment before and he had already turned off the amp, unplugged the guitar, and approached the counter. His eyes never left the guitar.

"So?" Bill asked in anticipation. "How is it?"

"It's perfect. I'll take it," he announced with his boyish smile.

"Sounds great!" Bill exclaimed. "I wish you weren't so hard on those guitars, but I do appreciate the business." Bill added with a chuckle.

"These cheaper off brand guitars seem to hold their own for a while. That's why I never buy the expensive ones," he answered with a smirk as he turned towards Lila to gauge her reaction.

Satisfied, Bill reached for the price tag to ring up the purchase. He looked down at the tag in his hands as he reacted the register and thought to himself for a moment.

"The price says $150, but since you are a frequent flyer around here, I'll throw in an old guitar bag and get you out the door for $100 even."

"That would be far to kind of you, you really don't have to do that," he protested.

"No, it's the least I can do for a good customer like you," Bill replied as he set a guitar bag on the counter next to the guitar.

Lila watched as the guitar was paid for and carefully zipped into its new home inside the bag. Then he courageously threw the strap over his head and the bag came to a rest on his back. Lila had been wondering what Bill meant about the guitars ever since he had first questioned it. There was still so much she did not know about him. As they walked out the shop and said their goodbyes to Bill, she wondered if she should ask him or wait until he was ready to explain it to her.

"What was the thing about the guitars?" Lila asked puzzled.

He laughed as she asked him because he knew that he would have to explain it sooner or later.

"Well sometimes I'm a little passionate when I play and I tend to be a little rough with my guitars. That's why I'm in there so often buying new ones," he said as he started his ritual with his glasses.

This did not help to explain anything to Lila. She now had way more questions than he had answers.

"You break your guitars? How does that even happen?" She asked with a shocked look on her face.

"I'll just have to show you sometime. It's kind of hard to explain," he said with a chuckle. "Anyways, why don't you take some pictures as we walk back to the car?" he added as an attempt to distract her.

Lila was still fixed on questioning him, but decided to save it for later. No use to keep pressuring him if he did not want to explain it to her. She was a very smart girl and she knew she would get her answers out of him sooner or later. This made her happy thinking she was smarter and more devious than him.

She pulled the camera and the box of film from the bag.

"Hold this," she commanded as she handed over the empty bag. And quickly went to work loading the film into the camera with the focus and precision of a surgeon. The camera clicked and popped as everything fell into place and he was very impressed how quickly she was able to load the film.

"Lets see if it will take a picture. We won't be able to see the picture of course, but if the shutter seems to work and it cycles to the next negative in the film strip then there's a chance it may work," she said excitedly. Lila stepped back and focused the camera on the blonde haired boy with his mirrored sunglasses, the very worn flannel jacket hanging from his shoulders and the newly purchased guitar on his back. It was the first time she had seen him shy as he nervously played with his hair. A slight shade of redness came to his cheeks as he blushed. She snapped the picture without hesitation.

"Why are you being so shy?" she asked with a giggle. She thought it was cute how he acted.

"I don't know. I didn't expect you to take my picture." He laughed as he added, "I thought you were going to creep up on strangers and take their pictures."

Lila smirked with a playful anger in her eyes. "Oh shut up!" she finally announced as she gently slapped him on the arm.

He just laughed it off thinking of himself as being incredibly funny. She grabbed his hand as they walked down the street. What could be more perfect, he thought. She has her camera, I have my guitar and in the moment the world is ours because we have each other.

He admired the architecture as they passed the tall buildings downtown. Occasionally, she would let go of his hand to snap a photo here and there of whatever caught her attention. He thought it was fascinating to watch the way she moved and twisted to get just the right angle for her shot, at times half running, half dancing back and forth across the sidewalk in front of him just to get the perfect angle. She took pictures of the buildings, parking meters, and alleyways, whatever seemed to catch her attention in the moment. And he loved every minute of it. They rounded the last corner and headed towards the parking lot where the car was left. Lila felt a surge of excitement as she thought about the adventure that could lie ahead.

She looked up at him with her big alluring eyes, "What's on the agenda now?" She had such sweetness in her voice as she asked the question.

He knew he could not get enough of this girl, and he was sure she felt the same for him. He knew she would follow him anywhere, as he would follow her to the edge of the earth.

"I have an idea. There's a levee on the delta not too far away from here," he declared. "It may be a good place to take some pictures. Would you like to go?"

Lila had been waiting patiently for his idea. She already had the answer to his question long before he asked it.

"That sounds like fun!" she exclaimed as she grabbed the handle to the passenger side door of the car. "I'll let Stacy know that we're done with breakfast and I'll be staying for a while longer."

Pleased with his idea, he opened the driver door and climbed in. The orchestra of a vehicle began again. Stomping his feet on the clutch, brake and gas, the rhythmic rumble of the car came to life under his command as he took off down the street working through the gears.

This time Lila knew what to expect as she watched him, adoring every moment of it. His hand brushed her thigh in between shifts as she watched his golden blonde hair blowing in the wind coming through the window. In the sunlight, he glowed with an aura that engulfed his entire body. She marveled at the way he sang every song that came on the radio. Lila found it compelling that he always sang with a volume just under the radio so that if she really focused she could hear him. It was as if he was bashful to the sound of his own voice and feared someone might hear him singing.

"What are you staring at crazy?" he said in a playful tone, sticking his tongue out after he spoke.

"Oh nothing, just watching you." she replied with a charming smile.

He blushed as he tried to hold back a smile knowing it was a losing battle. He had been stealing glances in her direction the entire ride. Her eyes were full of mystery and excitement as he drove the car. Her smile was contagious as it produced a calm feeling through his soul.

The car turned onto the street leading towards the levee. The street turned and bent through some nice neighborhoods before coming to a dead end into a marina. Right before the end of the road, they turned onto a much smaller road that led them up a small hill onto the levee. This road was much rougher. The mustang twisted and turned, jumped and bucked over the bumps and holes in the pavement. Lila was a little nervous on this road, but he was not. In his mind, this was his road. He had come to know every single turn in and out over the years, and he was not afraid to drive fast. As they rounded the first turn the water was soon on their left with a ten-foot rocky drop off leading to it. Off to the right was at least twenty feet down to the farmland below.

"You aren't going to kill me out here are you?" Lila said half joking, half serious, as she eyed a screwdriver on the floor of the car.

He gave her a slight evil grin. "What do you think the shovel in the trunk is for?"

"What!" she said in shock as she grabbed the screwdriver. "What shovel?" she demanded as she tried to remember seeing a shovel in the trunk.

He let out a hysterical laugh. "Calm down killer, I'm just kidding!" he said reassuringly. "You'll be fine," he added as his eyes stayed focused on the road.

"That's not very funny mister," Lila declared with relief and she gave him a swift smack on the arm.

"Don't worry. We are almost there," he stated while still laughing to himself.

CHAPTER 4

The car slowed as it approached the place he wanted to park. He eased off the old beat up road onto the dirt shoulder near the drop off that led to farmland. There was just enough room for the car to make it off the road. They both got out and looked around admiring the beauty of the landscape. He explained to her that the river next to them was the deep-water channel and that large ships would come in from San Francisco all the way to the port of Stockton. He explained a little about the farmland and its rich soil which was excellent for growing crops because of the close proximity to the water. Having farmers in her family, Lila already knew about everything he was talking about. She found it cute the way he explained how crops worked so she decided not to interrupt him.

As this was being said, he was gently pulling his new guitar out of the backseat of the car and removing the case. Lila held her camera in her hands gazing around at all of the potential photographs. She had wandered a few feet away from the car and saw him sitting on the trunk of the car with the guitar propped against his knee. Not wanting to spoil the moment, she carefully raised her camera and while he was looking down tuning the guitar, took a picture without him ever knowing. Pleased with her accomplishment she turned and went about her business.

The sun was hanging high in the sky. The earth was warming up.

The full heat of the day was just a few hours away. As he finished tuning his guitar and started strumming along to the newly found beat of his heart, he watched Lila, marveled by her grace and elegance. This must be what it is all about, he thought to himself. Something out on the water caught his eye.

Boats had been racing about as they always do on a nice summers day. The weekends were always filled with fishermen or partiers; wake boarders or skiers, and just the kind of people who enjoyed the relaxing nature of it all. There was a local gathering place that everyone knew about called ski beach. Anyone was welcome and people from all walks of life and many different types of backgrounds all gathered together for a great time. The conversations could last hours with complete strangers while sharing food and alcohol. Everyone was always in a great mood and good vibes filled the air.

As Lila was lost in her world of imagination, she was unaware that he was trying to focus in on a particular boat. He was sure he recognized it, but it was just far enough away to still harbor some doubt. As it came closer, he realized his assumption was correct. The boat was towards the middle of the channel and from where he sat, he could see a few people standing on the back, trying his best to make out the faces and identities.

He was about to break the silence between Lila and him to point out the boat that happened to be traveling by, when he noticed the boat starting to turn towards the levee. Wondering why, he waited to see before he said anything.

A sharp crackling white noise boomed across the water as the loud speaker from the boat was turned on.

"You in the blue mustang!" the loud speaker announced. "Prepare to be kidnapped!"

Lila's eyes widened. Her heart sank for a moment, as she was stunned by the statement from these strangers. She stood frozen in place as she tried to piece together the scene before her, watching intently as to what could be happening, while clenching her camera with a death grip.

By this time, he was lying across the trunk with his back on the rear window of the car laughing hysterically. Tears filled his eyes as he watched Lila's reaction to the scene before her. He was still unable to control his breathing and laugher to let her know that everything was all right.

"What's going on?" she said in a rushed panic. Her arms were still frozen in place when the booming voice came over the water from the loud speaker once more.

"Lower the dingy!" the voice demanded. And as commanded, two men hoisted a small inflatable boat over the side of the yacht and lowered it into the water.

As this was happening, he rubbed his eyes to clear his vision and made cooing sounds to try to control his laughter. Finally able to breathe again he said with a big smile, "Don't worry Lila, I know them."

This set her at ease for the moment, just long enough to break free from her frozen state and walk back towards the car where he was still sitting.

"What's going on?" she asked once again, still confused at the sight unfolding in front of her.

"Well, It looks like we are going on an adventure," he stated in an excited tone.

This did not seem to settle Lila's wonderment. Still lost in her confused state, she could not help but just stand there as everything unfolded around her. She watched as he jumped off the back of the car and turned towards the door of the mustang. As she turned her focus back to the water, the small boat was now making its way to the levee they were standing on. Then she watched the yacht as it slowly circled in place waiting for its new guests to arrive. Still curious as to what he could possibly be doing in the car, she turned back to him as he pulled out a small speaker from behind the seat.

"I forgot I had this in here," he said with excitement. "It's a portable guitar speaker."

He was smiling as he turned it over in his hands searching for the

ON switch. Once it was located, he flipped the switch to test the battery strength. Satisfied, he flipped the switch once more and reached back into the car digging through his guitar bag. Within a moment, he revealed a guitar cable that was neatly wrapped and started stuffing it down into his pocket. He quickly grabbed his phone to check the time and send out a quick text message. Once this task was complete, he carefully closed the door to the car and walked back to where Lila was standing. Lila was furiously texting Stacy as he approached her. Still sensing her unease with the situation, he stood face to face with her, guitar still in one hand, and with the other he clipped the small speaker onto his belt without ever looking down. Slowly, he removed his glasses to reveal his eyes once more to her.

"It's just some friends from high school," he stated as he tried to comfort her. "They are a lot of fun to be around."

Lila was gazing into his eyes the way she had the first time she saw them. The camera rested at her side as she fixed the lanyard around her neck. A smile formed across her face as she took a deep comforting breath. There was warmness in his eyes that Lila could not get enough of. It was as if all her fears and worries fell away and all that was left were love and happiness.

"You could have at least given me a heads up!" she announced in a snappy playful voice.

They stood there together in the moment, eyes fixed on one another. The world fell away. Nothing else mattered as they each studied the other's face, waiting for any type of sign of what to do next. Even the rays of sunlight beating down on them, on this now very hot day, did not seem to distract their focus. He studied the soft curves of her cheeks as they effortlessly flowed into her adorable little nose and down to her delicate lips. She slowly bit her bottom lip in anticipation of a kiss. Her mind raced as she imagined what his lips would feel like on hers, how his skin would feel pressed against her own.

He was not sure what sign he was looking for, but when he saw it, he was certain at that moment he knew. Gently, he placed his hand with the sunglasses still in his palm, around her waist and pulled her closer to him. He studied her eyes for any sign of protest, but there was none. Instead he was greeting with warm wanting eyes. Slightly scared, and definitely full of nerves, he leaned forward for a kiss. Trying to contain her excitement, she held her breath as she pushed her toes against the ground to raise her body to meet him. Her lips were almost to his.

"You better bring that guitar you fucker!" the voice from the loud speaker echoed across the water shattering the moment like an atomic bomb.

Both of them stood there in disbelief and embarrassment as they each reacted in opposite ways. Lila looked down and away to hide her blushing face from his. He looked up trying his best not to burst out with laughter. Both of them wondered how the timing of the loud speaker could have been so perfect to ruin such a moment.

Lila finally gathered her composure long enough to look back up at him as he said, "Come on, you ready to go on an adventure?"

"Yes," she replied, with a slight smirk on her face hiding her true intentions.

The dingy had crashed against the rocks of the levee. Timothy Reed had been driving the boat and still sat next to the small engine at the back. Timothy had red curly hair just long enough to cover the tops of his ears. He was the type to grow his hair out during the summertime until it turned into a bushy red afro with all the curls and locks. He always kept it around a medium-short length during the rest of the year. He wore bright green and blue board shorts and a t-shirt with a surfer logo on it. He was always very casual, but could dress up when needed to. Timothy lived with James and paid rent for one of the rooms in James' house. The two of them were always inseparable and constantly finding themselves in mysterious situations. Timothy was by far the calmer of the two, but he had no problem holding his own when James came up with one of his wild ideas.

James Cotton was lying in the front laughing at the crash and astonished at his ability of not spilling a drop of beer throughout the event. James was the wild and crazy party animal. If alcohol was around, James was always close by. He had short dirty blond hair and wore a constant grin as if he was always plotting some big idea. He had on a Bob Marley t-shirt that seemed to be one size too big for him and red board shorts. James always craved attention, and in doing so, always had to prove he was the craziest in any situation. After high school, his grandparents had retired and moved down to Long Beach leaving him their old house, which he used for non-stop parties. His only roommate was Timothy, even though it was a two-story three-bedroom house. The extra room was usually left for anyone who needed a place to sleep after a long night of partying, and with his family's money, there was no need to rent it out.

Unaware of what had taken place on the levee, Timothy finally called out, "You guys ready or what?" James and Timothy laughed and joked while they waited for a response to come shouting down back to them.

"Let's go on that adventure," he replied, anguishing in the missed opportunity.

He placed the sunglasses back over his eyes. His protective barrier from the world was now back in place. They walked hand in hand across the old broken road and started down the side of the levee. He helped Lila carefully over the sharp uneven rocks and protected his guitar, pulling it in close to his side. As they reached the boat, James stood up to greet his guests. Introductions were made as he helped Lila onto the boat.

"Hi, I'm James, and this is Tim," James announced proudly.

"It's very nice to meet you, I'm Lila," she responded in a respectful manner as she found a seat in the small boat.

"What's up guys?" he asked the gentlemen in the boat as he climbed in.

"Just enjoying the weekend as always," Timothy responded as James carefully took a sip of his beer.

James held the beer like a trophy in front of him, "Check it out! I didn't even spill a drop, even with Tim's dumbass driving," he said with a grin.

"I wouldn't expect any less," he proclaimed as he found a place in the front of the boat to sit down.

Timothy fired up the engine on a swift pull of the starter rope and they took off back over the water towards the mother ship. Timothy was a little wild and sporadic in his movements, causing a gentle mist to overcome the front of the dingy.

Protecting the guitar from the water he yelled out, "Be careful of the guitar!"

The engine roared across the water as the dinghy made its way to the yacht. Lila tucked her camera under her arm to avoid any unwanted moisture to come in contact with this precious instrument.

"Sorry man! We're almost there!" Timothy replied.

As they neared the rear deck of the yacht, Lila could see the rest of the welcoming party, which consisted of three girls and the driver of the boat. She studied the girls. All three of them were blonde and in bikinis, and other than the color of their bikinis, at first glance she could not tell them apart.

All four in the dingy carefully climbed out of the boat and onto the back deck. Lila was introduced to the new faces that had been standing on the boat awaiting their arrival.

"Hi, I'm Kate, and this is Katelyn, that's Katherine, and this is Greg," she announced as she finished pointing at the driver.

Kate had the body of a gymnast, barely hidden under a bright blue bikini. She was petite and slender. Her long blonde hair hung down to her lower back, which she was very proud of and rarely put up. Kate was much calmer than the other girls and very level headed. She was also much smarter than the other girls as she was on her way to become a registered nurse. Attending college at Sacramento State, she was able to come home just about every weekend.

Katelyn was full of energy and the most easy-going. She was the type of person who could get along with anyone and genuinely enjoyed being surrounded with company. Her job as secretary for a car dealership suited her perfectly. Katelyn had warm soft brown eyes that greeted any and everyone. Her sandy blonde hair was not as long as Kate's, as she wore it just past her shoulders. She was adored by all for her happy-go-lucky personality.

Katherine was the only one of the three who had wavy blonde hair that she usually had in a braid of some type and was always changing her hairstyle. She was definitely the wildest of the three and got along with James and Timothy very well in that sense. Not afraid to jump into any situation, she was ready for anything, especially when she was drunk. There were many stories of her drunken encounters, but it never seemed to bother her and she wore it with pride.

Lila was slightly overwhelmed with all the new names she had just learned in the past few minutes. "It's very nice to meet all of you," she replied.

While the introductions were being made, he had set his guitar down on a chair off to the side and carefully placed the speaker next to one of the legs. Then he made his way down the line, starting with shaking hands with Gregory. After a quick hello, and comments about how good it was to see one another, he made his way to the girls, hugging each one with a big embrace. Lila studied how they interacted with him. Each one was fixed on watching his every move as he proceeded from one to the next.

"It's so great to see you," they each said in their own way, slightly out of unison. Lila studied patiently, trying to unravel the mystery of their relationship.

Timothy and James struggled to pull the dingy back onto the boat into the place it once sat. Timothy was bent far over the railing pulling with all his might. James still had the beer in his hand and lent an unhelpful hand to the cause.

Frustrated, Timothy yelled at him, "Put that fucking beer down already and help me."

"Do I have to do everything around here? Shit," James replied jokingly as he set his beer down gently and gave a better effort.

"*You* do everything around here? Oh yeah, I'm sure," Timothy stated sarcastically.

The boat was finally pulled up over the rail and set gently down by the two men. Pleased with their work, James grabbed his beer and finished the last of it.

"C'mon, let's go drink some beer," James said proudly looking over their accomplishment.

As they rounded the corner to the back deck, everyone was seated, already in full conversation. Gregory and the girls were sitting around a half moon bench with a table in front of them. The guest of honor and Lila were seated on a long bench at the back of the boat, just a few feet away from the table. Timothy and James sat down on the bench between Lila and an ice chest sitting on the deck. James rubbed his hands together like a master of a craft ready to indulge into a work of art. He opened the lid of the ice chest and asked everyone if they had any preference on which alcohol they would like. Pleased with the answers he received, he started the process of passing out the liquor. The girls wanted the fruity drinks, tall cans of Strawberitas. Gregory asked for a light beer. Timothy wanted a heavier darker beer and James just grabbed the closest one to his hand for himself.

"Why aren't you drinking?" James asked him.

"I have to drive later, so I'll just have one or two when we get to the beach," he responded. "But I'm sure I'll be drinking with you guys tonight."

James said excitedly, "That's for sure! It's always a party when you come back into town."

He laughed as he replied, "But I'm here almost every weekend."

"So! There's still always a party," James added as he cracked open his beer. "Are you going to play your guitar already?"

He laughed as he stood up to retrieve his guitar. Once he had the amp and guitar back in his possession, he began the process of connecting the cable that he pulled from his pocket.

"Shouldn't you be driving the boat?" he asked Gregory, realizing that everyone was sitting on the back of the boat.

"I dropped an anchor while they were picking you up. So play a song already!" he said with a quick and witty reply.

Gregory came from a very wealthy family. If someone could not figure that out from the fancy yacht and cars he drove, as well as the way he dressed, he was sure to tell them. Though he was the quietest of the group, he had a way with the ladies. He kept himself well manicured and his hair always as perfect and professional as possible. Even on a day like today, he wore a collared shirt with white and blue stripes and matching shorts. On his yacht, he always had his Sperry Top-Siders on as well. He was not so much snobbish as he was more confident. Gregory was easy to be around and was always ready whenever it came to fun.

The guitar rang out and filled the air just like everyone had anticipated. After a few chords of an intro, he began singing as the entire crew erupted into a choir of voices. Singing and excitement filled the air. Lila did not know the song and watched in amazement, as everyone around her knew every single word. She wondered how she had never heard of it before. The melody was so smooth and catchy that it left her puzzled.

As the song ended, everyone burst into a fit of clapping. He could not do anything but sit there and say thanks to everyone. Lila admired the situation. She could sense his almost uncomfortable dilemma as in the way someone feels helpless while people are singing Happy Birthday to them.

Before Lila could ask what song it was that he had just played, Katherine blurted out, "How long have you two known each other?"

He sat there now even more shyly. "We met this morning on the train," he finally responded.

Laughter and shock shot out around this newly formed crowd as questions filled their heads.

"Damn you work fast!" James blurted out without hesitation.

"Shut up James!" Katherine demanded as she scowled at him. "I think it's sweet," she added lovingly with a hint of jealousy in her heart.

The men wanted to know all of the dirty details. The women were jealous to hear the romance that must have taken place, as well as the dirty details. Katherine and Gregory smiled at one another as if they knew their plans connected in their heads.

"I'm going to need all of your guys' help to get this boat underway," Gregory announced.

"Lila, why don't you come with us, we'll show you around the cabin," Katherine added, as the plan was executed perfectly.

Without a protest, Lila was whisked away by the girls into the cabin, while the gentlemen went to the top deck. She followed them through a sliding glass door and down two steps into the cabin. The inside of the yacht was magnificent with everything expected with a luxury lifestyle. A rather large galley for a boat was just off to the side of the door, complete with granite counter tops. Just beyond the galley sat a large sofa under glamorous windows cased in gold trim. A dining table big enough to fit in a house sat to the left of the door with intricate patterns carved into the wooden top. Along the wall beyond the table hung a fifty-inch flat screen television between perfectly spaced portholes. An elegant white carpet covered nearly the entire floor, except of course, the inlaid tile throughout the galley.

"So, tell us everything!" Kate said with intrigue and envy in her eyes as the girls took a seat around a table downstairs. The soft white lights in the ceiling illuminated their faces in such a way as to almost glow.

Lila laughed, "There's not much to tell really. We met this morning, he took me to breakfast and we bought a guitar, then out to here." She tried to downplay the events of the morning as she said them while she gently removed the camera from around her neck and placed it off to the side of the table.

"No way. Tell us everything. There's always more to it then that. There has to be *way* more than that," Kate said as she pushed for more details.

Katelyn asked exactly how they met and so Lila started the story from the beginning. All of the girls listened intently and clung to every word as if they wished the story were about them personally. As it went on, each one of the girls took turns asking her to elaborate different details. Their excitement grew the more they learned.

As this was taking place down stairs, a different version of the same story was being told upstairs. The men did not care for all the silly details. They just wanted a play by play of what happened. He told the facts as if reciting the highlights of a baseball game on the evening news and the men were content.

"So you gonna bang her?" James asked after the events were stated.

"Dude, I just met her," he replied with a laugh.

"Didn't you almost make out with her? And you met her like 5 hours ago," Timothy added.

He sheepishly replied, "Well, yeah, but. . ."

Gregory butted in, "They'll definitely bang. That girl is so fucking hot!"

He didn't respond to the comment other than a laugh.

Downstairs was still going much smoother than the gentlemen's conversation. Katelyn had pulled out a little bag from her purse, but had yet to open it. As Lila talked, she was still studying these girls through their questions and comments. The only thing she knew about them was that they all went to high school together. It was very clear to her the bond they all had, but there was also something more she could not quite place. Maybe if she asked some questions she could find out more about them, and him.

"All of you have known him for a long time, and I just met him today. What is he like?" Lila finally asked, dying to know as much as she could about him.

Kate was quick to answer, "He has always been an amazing person. He's smart, funny, super cute, of course you know that part, and talented . . ." she continued on and on, reminiscing the thought of him as if she were trapped in a daydream.

Lila listened attentively as Kate spoke. She was definitely getting the feeling there was now much more to the story. She thought about how the more she learned of him, the more questions were left unanswered. What a mystery of a person she thought to herself as each girl took turns describing the boy Lila had spent the day with. She still had not learned much, even after all of their explaining and it was becoming painfully confusing. Lila had wanted to dig deeper, but this was not exactly what she had in mind.

While the conversation turned into bickering back and forth between Kate and Katherine, Katelyn had removed the contents of the bag by pouring them onto the table. Like a mad scientist, she carefully cut the contents with a credit card into smooth even lines. Even taking care to see that every speck of the white powder was packed tightly together. Once this chore was done she licked the end of her finger and carefully ran it over the edge of the card. Nothing was to go to waste. Lila had been so focused on how funny the conversation between the two girls had been that she had not paid any attention to what was taking place. Katelyn rolled a twenty-dollar bill nice and tight in her fingers and held it proudly as she looked over her handy work. Lila had asked if he had ever had a girlfriend and so by this time they were deep into the story that very few knew. He had a few they told her, but the important one was his last one. It had happened a few years before, Lila was told. She also learned that it had ended badly. More intriguing to the story was how he had reacted after it was over. Katelyn hit a line that she had prepared which brought everyone's attention to her. The other girls were excited because they wanted some as well. Lila was terrified. She had never seen someone snort cocaine before.

"He started partying a lot and he got a little wild for awhile," Katelyn announced with her head tilted back letting the drugs take effect.

Now Lila was mortified. What was she to think of this guy she had barely met? If the girl in front of her, doing cocaine, said that he was wild, then what could that possibly mean about him? Lila finished her beer and grabbed another one from a stack that had been brought over to the table with them. She was not about to contemplate this sober.

The girls then went on about stories of him out partying and how he was always so charming and nice. At one point or another, it seemed they had all fallen for him to some degree. Maybe they still have feelings for him, Lila thought as she watched each girl take their turn with the lines on the table. Now that they were high, the conversations escalated in speed and volume, but the content was shifted to more funny topics of his so-called crazy party stories. Even Lila was enjoying herself laughing and listening to all the ridiculous things he had done in the past.

"And that was the night where he climbed on a table, but was too drunk to even get off by himself, so he just laid there talking with an accent all night while everyone else had to keep getting beer for him!" Kate said, as her face was red with laughter.

Lila was offered a line and respectfully declined. The girls went about their business of taking turns amongst themselves while telling the stories. Once the cocaine was finished, Katelyn suggested that they go find the boys. The girls filed out of the cabin and onto the back deck before climbing the ladder onto the top deck. Lila found him standing there with the rest of the men and put her arms around him.

"I hope they didn't say too much about me," he said with a chuckle.

"Oh, I heard plenty," she said with a smirk across her face. "Especially all about how wild you can get."

He stood there in her arms with the look of embarrassment strung across his face while all of the other guys laughed.

"Yeah, he's one of the few that can out-drink a fish," James drunkenly blurted out.

"Shut up James!" he snapped quickly.

Gregory chimed in, "Yeah James, keep your mouth shut every once in a while."

He turned back towards Lila, "It was a long time ago, I promise." He waited to see what she would do next.

"That's ok," she replied. "I was a little wild too," she added with a wink.

His heart dropped as the thoughts raced through his mind as to what kinds of things she could have possibly done. She let him squirm within his own twisted ideas before finally coming to his rescue.

"I'm just kidding. I've never done anything close to the stories I've just heard," she finally stated.

Timothy butted in, "What's wrong? You worried that you might find a girl that could out-do you?"

"Leave him alone already. He's still sweeter than all of you assholes," Katherine said, coming to his defense. The girls had been listening to everyone gang up on him and snickering at their envious tone towards him.

"Yeah, yeah, yeah. Anyways, we are almost there," Timothy said as he pointed to the beach just up ahead.

CHAPTER 5

Everyone cheered, as they got closer to ski beach. He explained to Lila how fun and crazy it gets there in the summer when everyone shows up to party. There were already boats lined up across the beach and within the hour it would be full. When that happens, he explained, a second row would be started of boats backing in so that they were deck to deck with the first row. Music was already pouring out of every boat. The clashing songs created a loud inaudible noise that filled the channel. She asked him why they all play their own songs instead of one boat playing for everyone. He explained that since no one could ever agree on a song, they all played their own as loud as possible to show off their expensive sound systems and show off their music choices. Gregory found a spot next to all the ski boats at the far side of the beach and ran the boat aground.

"Land Ho!" Gregory cried out as everyone cheered once again. "Do any of you girls have an extra swimsuit for Lila?"

"I do!" Kate replied. "Follow me Lila," she said as she started down the stairs.

"I've got some extra board shorts for you as well, I'll go grab them," Gregory added as he headed down behind the girls.

As he followed Gregory through the boat he thanked him once again. Gregory found the extra board shorts and handed them over.

"No worries brother," Gregory stated as he patted him on the shoulder and left him to change down in the cabin.

He quickly changed into the board shorts and left his shoes along with his pants and shirt in a pile in the corner of the room, then made his way to the back deck. The sun felt amazing against his skin as he soaked it in, still rejuvenating from the night before.

Lila changed in the bathroom and quickly found the pile of clothes he had left behind. She added her clothes to the pile and headed towards the back deck. She could see him standing on the deck with his back towards her. As she stepped out of the doorway he turned around to greet her. He stood staring helpless at this beautiful goddess of a woman as she walked towards him. This was the first time he was able to see her body, only covered by a perfect black bikini that clung tightly to her figure, accenting it completely. Her delicate hair blew gently in the wind as she walked. Her stomach, so perfectly toned, was complete with a belly button piercing that bounced as she moved. Her legs were so long that he was unable to find the ends of them by the time she reached him.

As she was walking towards him, she admired his body. This was the first time seeing him without a shirt and jacket. The outline of a six-pack across his abs caught her eyes. She glanced across his broad chest and the defined muscles in his arms. She laughed a little as she saw the two toned blue swimsuit he was wearing, but quickly focused on the way his golden blonde hair moved in the gentle wind of the afternoon around his face. As she reached him, she pulled off the big shiny glasses from his face so she could look deep into his eyes once again.

"Are you going to pick your jaw up off the ground or should I grab it for you?" she asked innocently.

"Was it that obvious?" he replied with a laugh.

"Well, you may have been able to hide it if you weren't drooling everywhere," she added jokingly as she pretended to wipe his chin for him.

He smiled down at her. "You're a punk," he said with a grin pasted across his face.

She reached up and gave him a small peck on the cheek, handed the glasses back, and walked over to the ice chest. He watched as she slowly and melodically bent over to grab a beer out of the ice chest. After taking her time to select which one she wanted, she finally pulled one out and stood back up. In a slow seductive motion, she looked over her shoulder back at him and finished with a joyous little smile. Her eyes pierced his heart like cupid's arrow, as he stood there utterly speechless.

"Well, are you coming?" Lila asked as she made her way to the top deck to rejoin the group.

Her words snapped him out of his fantasy world and back into real life. He gathered his composer and followed her without saying a word. Once back on top, they took a seat with the rest of the group. He put his arm around her and pulled her as close as possible, still unable to speak. James was telling a story about some nonsense. Timothy was arguing with some of the details. Gregory was correcting them here and there. Katherine would chime in from time to time to add bits and pieces that they overlooked. Kate laughed at the commotion and Katelyn was setting up music on the yacht's stereo. Lila gazed around taking it all in. From person to person she scanned and watched how they all interacted with one another. Lila gazed out over the ski boats on the beach. He was right, she thought, as she watched a second row of ski boats filling in the lines. A country song came over the stereo joining the already busy air of sound. Lila recognized the song right away as Alan Jackson's Chattahoochee. James argued to put on a rap song that he wanted to hear. Katelyn said something along the lines of 'James was not in charge because he did not set up the music himself'. It was finally agreed upon, by Katelyn herself, that Timothy could choose the next song, not James.

Lila looked up at him and realized he had slipped back into his unbelievable world of thought. This time she just left him in it and sipped on her beer while he smiled at her. Lila tried focusing in on the conversation between Kate, Katherine, and Gregory, but even she was having a hard time keeping up. She was falling into a nice soothing buzz from the alcohol that was becoming peacefully relaxing.

Suddenly a voice shouted out from the side of the boat, "Is that who I think it is? Is that really who I think it is?"

The voice was sharp enough to cut through all the noise in the air. It shot past the conversations and the music like a bullet breaking through the bubble of his imaginary world before finally coming to a rest. He eased himself back to look over the side of the boat and saw a familiar face.

"The one and only baby!" yelling out his reply.

"Why didn't you tell me you were in town already?" the voice interrogated him.

"I just got in this morning, I hadn't had time yet. Wait just a sec, I'll be right down," and with that he jumped up from his seat and raced to the ladder to head down to the lower deck.

Kate saw Lila's puzzled look. "Yeah, he's kind of a celebrity whenever he's in town," she said with a giggle.

"Kind of?" Gregory chimed in. "That's a bit of an understatement."

They all watched as he ran back across the top deck to grab Lila. In the midst of his excitement, he had forgotten to ask her if she wanted to come along. She quickly agreed as he grabbed her hand to lead her down to the deck below. Once on the deck, he hopped over the rail and down into the waist deep water. She was a little reluctant at first to get wet, but he assured her that the water felt great. She calmly eased herself up and over the railing and he helped her down into the water. It was much better than she had expected. The water was a nice and cool temperature that seemed to be very refreshing, especially for this hot day. As Lila turned around, she was introduced to the man who had been yelling up to the top of the boat.

"This is Jeremy," he said as he introduced the man with the voice.

They each said their proper responses to the introductions.

"It's very nice to meet you." Lila said after she was introduced.

She had to lean in every time they spoke to try her best to catch a word here and there.

They made small talk for a few minutes about the weather and the summer. Jeremy had asked if he would only be in town for the weekend, even though he already knew the answer to that. Then Jeremy invited him to a party happening later that night and said that of course Lila was invited. He responded by saying that James was having a party and they should all meet up there later that night. Jeremy agreed with moving the party to James' because he had a much bigger house. They shook hands again and said how it was always good to see each other and said their goodbyes.

"And it was very nice to meet you Lila," Jeremy added just before he left.

Lila replied, "It was very nice to meet you as well."

He grabbed Lila's hand after Jeremy had left. "Want to walk around and meet people?" he asked her with his loving smile.

"Yeah let's do it!" she responded quickly.

"This is always my favorite part," he told her. "I come out here a lot so I've made a bunch of friends. And there's a lot of people that I went to high school with that come out here as well."

Lila laughed, "Oh yeah, if you think you're such a big shot then let's see how many people you know."

He was excited for the challenge and gave a devilish grin. "Okay sweet thing, I'll show you a little of what I can do."

Lila followed him around for just about the next hour as they walked up and down the beach, in and out of boats. She could not believe what she was seeing. She had thought that his close friends were one thing, the way they treated him, but some of these people had to be complete strangers. No way did they all know him personally. But she was wrong. He was almost able to recite all the names of the people that they came across. Boat after boat was the same. All he would do was walk up to the boat and put his arms on the edge and wait. He had the element of surprise almost every time, hidden in all the noise and commotion around him. Finally someone would look over and get excited to see him. Then he would go through the process of shaking the guys' hands and hugging all the girls. He always remembered to introduce Lila as well. Small talk would ensue. They would have to get close and scream into his ear just so he could hear them. Most of the time Lila could not hear any of it with all the noise around, and he would move onto the next boat starting the process again.

From time to time, Lila would stand there taking in the scene that acted out around her. People and boats were everywhere and she was right in the middle of it. He had told her it was a crazy wild party, but nothing had really prepared her for this. She was overcome with excitement. It was all around her. It filled the air right along with the blaring music from boat to boat. People were drinking and dancing. Laughter and conversations sprang from every which way. No matter where she looked, there was just pure ecstasy in the moment.

Her beer had been finished for some time now and she had been carrying around an empty can. He leaned over and asked her if she wanted another one. Without hesitation, she agreed. He turned back to the boat he had been leaning up against and waved his arm in the air. A girl that Lila had not seen yet stood up and walked over to an ice chest. She was a beautiful blonde woman, maybe mid twenties at most, and the smallest thong bikini Lila had ever seen. She was engulfed in the site in front of her eyes as she watched the woman bend over into the ice chest, exposing way more than necessary. She then got up, dusted the ice from the top and made her way to the edge of the ski platform where Lila was standing in the water. Squatting down, almost pushing her chest into Lila's face, she handed the beer over to her. Somehow through all the shock and excitement of seeing this girl in front of her, she was still able to thank her before the woman stood back up and walked back to her seat.

"This place is amazing!" Lila screamed into his ear.

He had to turn his head close to hers just to say something back. "I know!" is all he could get out.

She followed him around from boat to boat a little while longer before he asked if she was ready to go back. Back at their boat, he had to hoist her up so she could grab the railing and pull herself over. He handed her beer up to her that some innocent bystander had to hold onto for a moment. Then he jumped up and grabbed the rail and in a sweeping motion threw himself over and onto the deck. He quickly noticed that his guitar had been left close to getting wet on the back deck of the boat and casually grabbed it as he started to make his way towards the top deck behind Lila.

"Are you getting hungry?" He asked. "I think they should have some food ready by now."

"Yes I am! But there is something you have to do first," she stated, still not ready to reveal herself.

Confused, he asked, "What is it?"

Excited that he could not figure out what was about to happen she replied, "You better kiss me already."

His eyes filled with joy. His heart skipped a beat. His hand gripped tightly around her waist. His lips yearned for hers. She waited patiently for his response. Once again, they were thrown into their own world. This time there was no fear or doubt in his mind as he leaned in towards her. She stood on the tips of her toes rising up to meet his lips. As they kissed, it was as if fireworks were going off right about their heads. A shower of sparks rained over them. Birds sang along to the violins in the distance. He could not even feel the ground under his feet anymore. There was nothing left of the world except for what he had in his hands, the girl and the guitar. She wrapped her arms around him, squeezing as tight as she could, never wanting to wake up from this dream. And in that moment, they were one.

They worked their way back up to the top where everyone was still sitting around. Their blushing smiles were plastered across their faces. Luckily for them, everyone was too drunk to notice. Gregory saw them coming. He jumped up and walked over to a small grill with smoke billowing out of the sides.

"You guys ready for some hotdogs?" he asked as he lifted the lid to expose the prize.

"That sounds great!" Lila exclaimed just realizing that she had not eaten since breakfast and had already had a few beers. She was feeling a little saucy now and thought food would be a good idea to sober her up a bit.

Kate and Katherine had already set out a whole buffet of food and as the hotdogs were ready, they prepared each one specifically for the person. Going around the circle, they took requests and even served them individually. Only after everyone was set with their meal, they finally sat down and started eating.

"So Lila, how did you like it down there?" James said with a mouthful of hotdog.

"Yeah, did you enjoy all the craziness?" Katelyn added.

Lila's face lit up as she marveled in the ecstasy that she felt while down in the middle of it all. "It was amazing! And wild!" she was at a loss of words to describe what she had seen.

The group started laughing. They all understood without her having to explain it.

"What was the craziest thing you saw?" asked Timothy.

"There was a lot! I've never seen in person some of the swimsuits I saw today. I didn't know they even made thongs that small. I swear some were just strings," Lila relived the excitement as she told the story. "And not to mention, he talked to just about every single person out there!" she added as she pointed to him.

"Yeah well, everyone seems to just flock to him," Katherine jokingly replied.

"Yeah, we still can't figure that one out," James said sarcastically.

He had been silently eating his hotdog and watching the conversation go on around him. Every once in a while, he gave a closed mouth smile to one of them while his mouth was full of food. He was so excited that Lila was having a great time. Nothing could have made him happier.

When he finally had a chance to chew his food all the way, he asked, "What time is it?"

"It's about three o'clock right now. What time do you need to be in?" Gregory asked.

"We should probably head in around five so it doesn't get too late," he replied while wiping mustard off his face.

"Yeah, that'll work out perfectly," Gregory agreed. "It takes awhile for this old beast to get back to the marina."

Katelyn stood up after finishing her meal and was hard at work on her next science experiment. After the conversation was over, she turned around and presented a tray full of shots. Cheers rang throughout the group as she made her way around the circle passing them out.

James asked Katelyn after she sat back down with a shot glass in her hand, "What would you like to toast too?"

Katelyn thought for a moment then said, "Raise your glasses in the air!" Everyone raised a glass. Katelyn continued, "To another wonderful summertime and great friends!"

The glasses tipped back and were poured into the mouths of the awaiting baby birds. Cringed looks and contorted faces, followed by cheers and laughter filling the scene. Soon the stereo was back on and the lunch intermission was over. The nonsense conversations started up again like a race car revving its engine and everyone joined in. James fell over out of his seat from laughing, beer still intact in his hand. Everyone celebrated as if it were a great achievement. Kate had found a captain's hat that was lying around and put it atop of Gregory's head. The drunker he got, the more crooked the hat sat as his sunglasses slowly slid off his face. Kate and Katherine were dancing to the music. The more they drank, the closer they got and the wilder the dance turned into. Timothy was the only one paying attention to them. He had been in charge of the music, playing song after song of the ones he knew they really liked just to see what would happen. Katelyn was talking to Lila, jumping from topic to topic. She talked about some crazy parties that would be coming up throughout the summer, and wild times at parties she had already been too. Also informing Lila about how much fun she's going to have being with them.

James and Gregory finally snapped out of their drunken haze when they saw how close Kate and Katherine were becoming when they almost kissed one another. Never to let a moment go to waste, James jumped up and grabbed the bottle of vodka that was sitting next to the grill and started pouring shots directly into the girls' mouths. Then quickly grabbed a beer for chaser and poured it down so they did not have to stop dancing. Pleased with his work, he moved onto phase two of his plan. Under the steering wheel he found a box that he reached in to retrieve Mardi Gras beads. He held them up as they shined back at him with the reflection of the sun illuminated the smile on his face. Turning back towards the girls, he held the beads up high, presenting their prize.

"Would you ladies like some beads?" James asked the girls.

Everyone waited to see what would happen in anticipation. Timothy and Gregory were wide eyed with excitement. Lila was curious and excited as well as she squeezed his hand tight while she watched. He squeezed her hand back sharing the moment with her, but he already knew what was about to happen. Katelyn knew as well. She sipped her drink calmly and watched it all unfold. Katherine grabbed Kate's head and pulled her in for a peck on the lips. The small crowd erupted, enjoying every second of the show. Kate's eyes filled with shock and envy. Her mouth was wide open. She had wanted to do it to Katherine first, but she was beat to the punch. In a quick retaliation, She grabbed Katherine's face and pulled her in for another small kiss. They were both winners in James' mind and he soon rewarded them with their bounty. They danced around, putting on a show for everyone before Katelyn finally decided to calm them down.

"Alright, alright. Keep your tops on, we still have a long night ahead of us," she told the girls. "Let's head down and powder our noses," she added as she got up and headed down stairs. "Lila, you're coming too," she commanded.

The girls adjusted their bikinis and followed Katelyn without question.

As Lila got up, he stopped her for a moment and said, "She is right, there is a long night ahead of us, it would be a good idea to have some water."

"Alright," she said without protest as she leaned in and gave him a small peck on the lips.

He watched her as she walked away, stunned by the rhythmic sway of her hips.

James called out before Katelyn had a chance to escape inside the boat, "Katelyn! Can I have some too?"

"Yeah, I'll bring you up some," she yelled back as she disappeared into the boat, the other girls quickly following her.

High fives were handed out to James from all around as well as praise on a job well done. A smile sprang across his face as he sat gloating in his achievement.

"Thank you, thank you. But really I couldn't do it without, my absolute awesomeness," he announced as he stood up and took a bow.

"Yeah, yeah, but remember what this guy right here can talk girls into when he has a little alcohol," Gregory added as he pointed across to him.

He sat there laughing with his drink in his hand, "Hey, that was a long time ago."

"Not so long ago if I remember correctly," Gregory snickered back. He raised his glass and personally toasted him.

Timothy finally spoke up, "We can't all be as lucky as you, but luckily we've been around long enough to reap the benefits of your exploits!"

They all raised their glass in another toast to him. Gregory leaned back behind his chair and pulled out a tray loaded with the essentials. A nice pile of weed, two blunt wraps, a lighter, and rolling papers. A pipe clung to the edge of the tray as he began to roll one of the blunts.

"But now he's got a new girl, so no more wild times for him!" James exclaimed to the group. "You better not let this one go, she's nuts about you. Have you seen the way she looks at you? Holy shit man, holy shit," James said directly to him.

"Yeah I know, there's something about her that's pretty special," he replied as he thought back over the day. "And I can't get enough of her either, it's amazing."

"For a guy that can get any girl in the world, you really did hold out for one hell of a chick," Gregory stated as he carefully packed the blunt.

Down stairs in the cabin the girls were all sitting around the table once again. Lila had a glass of water and a beer sitting in front of her. Katelyn was busy with her credit card shaping out lines. Kate and Katherine were talking about how perfect Lila and him looked together, gawking at the sights they saw earlier in the day of them sitting close to each other.

"Did you see the way he stares at you?" Katherine exclaimed.

Before Lila could even answer, Kate cut in, "I know! I've never seen him give that look to anyone before. It was like he looks at you and gets lost in his own world for a while."

"I think that's exactly what it is!" Katherine realized. "I tried asking him a question and he was so zoned out with that goofy smile that I finally gave up."

They all giggled as they remembered the moment it happened. Lila had already had a full glass of water and was working on her second one in between sips of beer. She had done exactly what he asked because she was still very curious as to what they could possibly be talking about when they casually mentioned the long night ahead. She had already had such a great day, how could it get any better, she thought to herself. She had lost track of what Kate and Katherine were saying and she watched as Katelyn put the finishing touches on her masterpiece. With the bill rolled tight, Katelyn hit her line and passed the bill to Kate who did not even slow down in her conversation while she took her turn. Neither did

Katherine as she dove nose first into the table. Lila laughed as she watched intently how each girl had her own reaction to the drugs. Katelyn always tilted her head back as if to let the high seep down her spine. Kate always rubbed her nose and breathed in extra hard to get every last bit in place. Katherine would pinch her nose and control the air intake by releasing and pinching again over and over in intervals.

"What's happening tonight?" Lila finally asked.

The girls looked at one other and giggled.

"Don't worry, you'll see," Kate finally spoke up after a moment. "There's going to be a really fun party that we will all go to."

Lila still lost in her confusion stated, "Everyone keeps saying that, but that doesn't really tell me anything. I feel like all day long I'll find out little tiny bits of information, but it just leads to more and more questions left unanswered." She seemed frustrated as she said it.

Kate spoke up once again, "Have you ever thought that maybe, that's exactly what he wants?" She waited a moment for Lila to let it sink in.

"How is that possible?" Lila questioned. "How could he control what I'm thinking?"

"Think about it," said Kate. "He's told you just enough about him so that you have a decent idea of the person he is, but at any point, he hasn't gone into any great details of his past or who he is right now." Kate watched as Lila worked over the information in her mind. "He's a very unique person to say the least, and when he's ready, he'll tell you everything. He'll open the doors to his world and let you walk right in. You just have to be patient."

Lila pondered it for a while. It was not exactly the answer she wanted to hear, but it did make some sense after all. "I think I'm falling for him which is insane because I just barely met him, and I don't know anything about him. Yet, I feel I've known him my entire life. Is that weird?"

Katherine took her turn stepping up to the plate on this one, "Girl, you already fell and you don't even know it yet."

All the girls laughed at the comment and took a moment to relax and sip on their drinks. Lila gazed out the window remembering that this massive party surrounded them. The music from the boats sent tremors through the water, shaking the bottom of the yacht. She realized that she had gotten so used to it that she had no longer felt the soft vibrations until she concentrated on them.

Finally breaking the silence, Katelyn asked, "What's that silly thing he always says?" She thought about it for a moment then answered herself, "Oh, I remember. It's his world, we are just living in it."

All of the girls laughed and headed back up to the top deck. Katelyn carried a CD case that she had prepared for James. As they climbed up, Gregory informed them that it was getting close to 5 o'clock and they were getting ready to leave. Once all the girls had taken their places, and James was taken care of, Gregory handed the blunt over to Timothy and instructed him to start the rotation. Gregory then fired up the engines. As soon as the blunt and the engines were ready to go, the boat reversed out of the beach, the blunt was passed, and they were off.

Lila had her hand embraced in his again and her head rested on his shoulder. He watched the boats on the beach as they passed by.

"Hey Greg, honk the horn a few times," he demanded.

"Sure thing," Gregory replied.

As the horn blasted out, they waved their goodbyes to the ski boats. With each blast, the crowd below screamed louder and louder as they waved. Everyone laughed at the sight before them. Lila, still lost in amazement with this person she just so happened to have stumbled upon, could not help but laugh along at the sight as well. He took his bows in a playful way along with Timothy and James, as the screams got louder and louder. He finally returned next to Lila's side.

"How do you do it?" Lila asked him.

"Do what?" he replied.

"You know exactly what I'm talking about," she said with light-hearted eye darts.

"I have no idea what you're talking about," he said with that childish grin on his face.

"You are so frustrating sometimes!" she had given up for the moment.

"I know," he said as he leaned over and kissed her on the cheek.

She rested her head on his shoulder as they watched the blunt pass from person to person. The rest of the group was lost in some deep conversation again. Lila glanced out over the water. It had a different shimmer to it with the sun deep in the evening sky. The trees on the levee swayed with the afternoon breeze. The farmland stretched beyond the levee almost as far as Lila could see. The fields had a beautiful green glow to them. She admired the contrast of colors before her. If I was a painter, I wonder if I could paint that, she thought. She studied the blues of the water, the sun's gold reflecting off the surface. She noted the white and grey of the rocks that lined the bank, the shades of brown and black within the levee and its road. The color of the leaves on the trees with their darkest of greens and the tan colors of the bark would bring a balance to the painting she thought. She gazed once more at the fields with its beautiful soft yellows and pastel green to make it stand out on its own and the sky with the silkiest of blues she had ever seen. I could paint that, she thought, what a lovely picture.

As she drifted into her daydream, she slowly slid down his body coming to rest with her head on his lap. He sat with one arm around her waist caressing her hand, slowly rubbing his fingers in patterns across hers. The other hand was gently playing with her hair, running his fingers through her plush locks. Even though the other girls were conversing amongst themselves, each one stole a glance at Lila. Envious of the way he treated her so different to anyone else. Why could that not be me, they thought, each one secretly jealous in her own way. Lila was unaware of any of this as she slowly drifted off to sleep.

"We are getting close," Gregory called out as he spotted the car on the levee. "Hey James, Tim, will you guys get ready to drop the dingy?"

"Aye Captain!" James yelled back as he sprang into action.

Timothy got up as well, but a bit more sluggish. He followed James down off the top deck to where the small boat was resting.

Lila had been asleep for only a few minutes lying in his lap, and he had the unfortunate task of waking her.

"Sweetheart, we're here," he called out in a soft calm voice as he slowly shook her arm.

Lila started to stir under him. He rubbed his hands lightly across her arms until she opened her eyes. As she awoke, Lila stared up at the big handsome man holding her.

"How long was I asleep?" she asked him.

"Only for a few minutes," he lovingly replied. "We have to run by my parents house for a little bit, but you can rest when we get there if you like."

"That sounds perfect," Lila said while releasing a yawn.

The boat came to a stop in the channel. Timothy and James worked quickly to lower the boat into the water. With the terrible coordination between the two of them, no one would have ever known they had done this multiple times.

While this was going on, Lila slowly got off his lap and to her feet. He walked cautiously behind her; worried that she may lose her balance in the hazy state she was in. They made their way down to the lower deck and into the cabin. Once the clothes were recovered, they quickly changed out of the swimsuits.

"I'm just going to change right here so don't stare at me," Lila giggled still in her drunken state.

Before he could even answer her, Lila had turned around and had her bikini top off. Trying his best not to stare, but being completely helpless, he watched the curves of her back as she gracefully moved. Trying not to be rude, he forced himself to shuttle his focus onto his own clothing. Out with the board shorts, and on with the pants in an effortless swoop. The shirt came next and he picked up the jacket to throw on his arms as well. He glanced over to see if she was ready.

Lila was moving slowly. She had a shirt on by now and had just pulled her tight pants over her hips. He studied the way her pants held tight to her legs as her loose wrinkled shirt swung loosely with her movements. Her hair bounced softly around her shoulders before she had the chance to pull the rogue strands from her face. And that was the moment he thought he was going to die. What he was witnessing was one of the sweetest, sexiest, most sensual moments of his life. Explosions, fireworks, parades, crowds cheering, were all happening in his head simultaneously. And he could not make a sound. He raised his hand to his mouth, clenching a fist and biting it was the only way to ensure not a peep of excitement escaped. He watched as she fixed her hair in slow motion. A quartet of instruments started in the corner of the room with Mozart's "Serenade for Winds". It was simply beautiful.

"Are you all ready to go?" Lila called out, breaking the fourth wall of his illusion.

"Yeah," he said in a raspy half broken voice. Clearing his throat he tried once more, "Yeah I'm ready."

Lila grabbed her camera off the table as he followed her out of the boat and to the awaiting chariot. The guitar and amp were gathered and tucked away safely. The crowd of friends gathered around to say their goodbyes. James helped Lila down into the boat and once she was settled, everyone else followed suit. Timothy ripped at the cord protruding from the engine and it let out a violent scream. Pulling away from the deck of the boat, the final goodbyes were cast and they were off.

Timothy tore across the water while James laughed with pleasure. Lila was just coming out of her haze for the moment as water splashed over the bow and a cool mist hit her face. Lila looked down where he lay, cradling his guitar, protecting it from the water. The trip was faster than before, Lila thought as the boat crashed up against the rocks and stopped with a sudden jerk.

"You're getting better at this Tim!" James cried out. "So when are we going to see you two again?" James added, as he shifted his gaze from Timothy to the two in the front of the boat.

"I think it starts at eight tonight, but I'll have to call and find out for sure," he replied as he carefully climbed out of the boat with his guitar.

Once stable, he turned and lent a hand to Lila as she delicately climbed over the bow and onto the rocks. As they started their climb up the levee, the small boat sped back off. Goodbyes were yelled once again over the roar of the motor. Reaching the top of the levee, he felt a peaceful easy feeling, as he knew his girl and his guitar were safe.

Lila noticed a few missed calls from Stacy and quickly called her back. "Yes I'm fine," she said into the phone. "We were out on a boat for a few hours... I'm still in Stockton... I'm going to stay for a while longer. I'll text you all about it in a bit."

"I feel so bad because she's been worried about me all day." Lila said as he put her phone away.

"Well, you did kind of run off with some strange boy," He joked.

As they reached the car, he gingerly placed his guitar in the backseat and pulled out his phone.

"I need to make a quick phone call to figure out the plan for tonight," he told her as she climbed down into the car.

A voice came through the phone, but it was too quiet for Lila to make out. She had awakened a little on the boat ride, but was still very much in a haze. Why on earth would these people keep wanting to party?, she thought. The voice on the phone must have been angry because from what Lila could hear, it sounded like the person was screaming. She watched his facial expressions for any indication to what could be happening. He sat there smiling and laughing, trying to get a word in here and there between screams.

"Do you need any help setting up? Or do you got this?" he asked the voice on the phone.

"Well yeah, I'm kind of with a girl right now," he said laughing, waiting to hear the reply.

He looked over at Lila to make sure she could not hear what was being said. "Oh shut up!" he snapped back into the phone, and then quickly covered his mouth so his laughter would not seep out.

"What time . . .What . . .What time is the . . .So it starts at eight? Eight-fifteen, but be there by eight? Ok, I got it," he said as he finally got the answer he was looking for.

"What starts at eight?" Lila asked, wondering why it was so specific.

"James is having the party tonight, but my friend Joe is always very meticulous about planning everything so he's usually put in charge of these types of things," he replied, assuring her it was nothing important.

As soon as the phone call was over, the car fired up and they were off down the broken levee road. His house was only a few minutes away and he was trying to get there quickly so Lila could rest. She was still trying to get comfortable in the seat as they pulled off the levee and onto the city street. Since the seat did not have a headrest, she had to slouch down and curl herself into a ball just to rest her head. Poor baby, he thought as he caressed her head in between shifts. He turned his attention back to the radio as Nirvana's "All Apologies" came on. He sang it softly to her as if he were trying to sing a baby to sleep. With the rumbling and bumping of the car, she could not get to sleep, but it felt so good just to have her eyes closed. The rumble of the engine was soothing as she lay there as if trying to sleep in a massage chair. As the car pulled into the driveway at his house, Lila slowly started the process of climbing back out. Her eyes were sensitive to the light as she tried to focus on her surroundings.

As she started to realize something she asked, "Are your parents home?" She panicked a little at the thought of meeting his parents while in a drunken haze.

He laughed as she struggled to walk around the car and he walked over to help her. "No, they are out of town this weekend," he finally replied as he helped her to the front door.

Once inside the house he helped her down the hallway and into his room. She was awake and alert as the bedroom light came on and she peered into the room. She walked in slowly and looked around, trying to take in as much information as she could. It was nothing like what she had expected.

Gazing from wall to wall she asked, "This is your room?"

"Yeah, this is where I grew up," he shyly responded.

Almost every inch of every wall was covered. The posters of musicians took up most of the space. Filling in the blanks were random pictures, drawings, and words in colorful sharpie. The entire room was one giant work of art. Lila was trying her best to take it all in. A poster of nuns smoking cigarettes with the caption, "Ash Wednesday" was hanging next to a Bob Marley poster. In between were actual photographs pinned to the wall of his friends and family. There was a colleague of photos that were put together creating the image of his mustang.

"Did you make that?" Lila asked, pointing to the colleague of the car.

"No I didn't. That was a gift from someone a long time ago," he replied while clearing his throat.

Lila sat on the bed and felt tired again. The room had been so amazing that she had not even looked down to see the line of guitars on stands along the wall. She counted five in front of her, two electric guitars, and three acoustic. One of the electric guitars had sparkle blue paint across its body while the other was a glossy black; similar to the one he had bought that morning. Two of the acoustic guitars were wood grain while one was slightly darker than the other. The third acoustic guitar had a beautiful reddish orange sunburst design across it. She lay down on the bed still admiring the artwork around the room.

"Get some rest, I'll wake you when it's time to go," he kissed her on the forehead as she closed her eyes, ready to sleep.

CHAPTER 6

After Lila fell asleep, he gathered some clothes and took a shower. He returned back to the room a few minutes later wearing a new pair of ripped jeans, a greyish-blue Cheech and Chong t-shirt and a blue flannel jacket. His appearance had not changed much from before. The indication of him even taking a shower was his long wet blonde hair, which he was carefully drying with a towel. He looked over at Lila and smiled. She seemed so peaceful resting in his bed. Once satisfied with his hair, he carefully picked up the glossy black electric guitar. Situated on the floor with his back against the bed and the guitar in his hands, he began the mundane task of cleaning his guitar. He gently wiped every inch with a soft rag and inspected it for any imperfections. He twisted the tuning knobs checking their smoothness, ran his fingers down the fretboard, making sure the frets were of even height. The volume knobs moved freely between his fingers. Then he systematically tuned it by ear, plucking the strings as soft as possible in order to not bother Lila. Once the guitar passed inspection, he moved onto the next and repeated the process. After his guitars were cleaned, he ran out to the car to retrieve the other two. Once again, he sat on the floor next to the bed where Lila slept and started his process once more. He could not help but think about the night ahead and how excited he was to have Lila come along. It was still crazy to him, he thought, we just barely met this morning, and already I feel like I've spent a lifetime with her. What are the odds that this amazing girl just happened to be sitting a few rows in front of me? If I had been in any other car on that train, we would have never met. This entire day would have never happened.

He was lost in thought until all the guitars were cleaned, tuned, and ready. Carefully, the electric guitars were placed into their individual bags and taken out to the car. He noticed that Lila's bags were still in the trunk and brought them in incase she wanted to change after her nap. Once back inside the house, he raided the fridge for food. A sticky note on the outside of the fridge said that the pizza was only a day old. He opened the pizza box to reveal that there was half a pizza left. Excited that he did not have to cook a meal, he heated up a few slices and ate. By now, it was getting close to the time they needed to leave. Lila had been asleep for around two hours and he hoped that she would be rested enough. He delicately climbed in bed beside her. Rubbing her arm and kissing her cheek. He attempted to wake her as gently as possible. She started to wake under his subtle hands, greeting him with a gorgeous smile on her face.

"How do you feel?" he asked her while gazing into her eyes. Lila's hair surrounded her face in a perfectly messy way.

"I feel rested, I'm glad I took a nap," she replied with her smile still across her face as she rubbed the sleep out of her eyes.

"Are you hungry? I can heat up some pizza," he added.

Lila stretched and let out a big early morning yawn. "Yeah, that'll be great."

He ran to the kitchen to heat up a few slices of pizza. By the time it was ready, Lila had moved to the edge of the bed. He came back in and handed her a glass of water and a plate of pizza. As she ate they laughed and joked about their day. She told him how she liked all his friends and they seemed really nice. She also could not get over the feeling of being in the water, in the middle of all those boats as the party went on around her. He laughed and said how he had gotten so used to it by now that he sometimes forgets how exciting it is to take a moment to look around. After she ate, he told her they had to leave in a few minutes, but she had enough time for a quick shower if she wanted. She promised it would be quick, and she would put her hair up so she did not have to wash it. His hair was almost completely dry by now.

She was in and out of the shower faster than he could ever imagine. So they had a few minutes to kill before they left. He wanted to be right on time, not too early. He laid on the bed and listened as Lila told stories of what happened with her and the girls downstairs. Going into detail about how shocked she was when Katelyn had pulled out drugs without saying a word. He thought it was funny how she had never been around things like that. He had been in so many situations that nothing scared him anymore.

Checking his phone he realized it was time to leave. "Are you ready to go?" he asked.

"Yeah I'm ready," she replied. They walked out of the bedroom, down the hall, and out of the house. Once in the car she asked, "So, where exactly are we going?"

"You'll see in about fifteen minutes," he smirked as the car rumbled to life beneath them.

"You haven't told me all day and you won't even tell me now?" Lila questioned in her frustration.

With a chuckle he replied, "If I've kept it a secret all this time, why would I tell you at the last minute before you find out on your own?"

"You are so frustrating sometimes!" she laughed as she gave him a kiss on the cheek while he drove.

He looked at her with his evil smirk, "It's my world, you're just living in it."

She could not remember if she was warned, or just told about this part, while the conversation started coming back to her. Stay patient, she remembered, stay patient, she thought. The radio had been turned down to a low whisper while Lila had been resting. As a recognizable melody slowly reached Lila's ears, she turned the volume up to the sweet surprise of Lit, "My Own Worst Enemy".

He bobbed his head along to the aggressively smooth guitar riff as the stick shift was slammed in and out of gear in timing. They were almost downtown and she recognized it from earlier that morning, but now the buildings were lit brilliantly as the sun set over the city. The mustang made a few quick turns this way and that, while zigzagging the streets. Lila realized something big was going on because the further they drove, the more parked cars there were on the street. Finally, they slowed down in front of a giant building that seemed to be brighter than the rest. The marque hanging off the building said that the show was tonight, but Lila did not recognize any of the band names.

"Are we going to a concert?" she asked excitedly.

"Yeah! See, I knew you would figure it out!" he said, feeding off her excitement.

"Why couldn't you just tell me that in the first place?" she was still puzzled as to why it had been kept a secret.

"Where's the fun in that?" he replied jokingly as he pulled the car into an alleyway that led to the back of the building. He finally stopped the car next to a back door that had a sign clearly stating 'No Parking'.

"We can't park here," she said after reading the sign.

"Then let's hurry and not get caught!" he said quickly as if he were being serious. "Can you help me with my bags in the backseat?"

Lila turned around and saw the four guitar bags in the backseat. He reached in and grabbed two while she grabbed the other two. Lila was in a slight state of shock carrying the guitars as they walked to the door in front of the car. She could hear music pulsing through the walls. As the door opened they were greeted with an overwhelming amount of sound. Lila was in absolute awe as she watched people running about. A girl with a clipboard ran over to them. Her dark hair, with purple highlights, was pulled back into a ponytail bouncing about as she moved. The glasses she peered through clung tight to a scowling distasteful look on her face. With a dark blue button down shirt, she seemed very professional and attractive the way it clung to the curve of her body.

Through a headset and over the radio she announced, "He's here!" She still wore a very displeased look on her face. "Where the hell have you been?"

"What?" he replied sarcastically. "I'm on time, there's still a few minutes before we go on."

A tech came from around the corner and took three of the guitars. "They should be tuned, but double check." Pointing to his newest guitar he added, "This black one is in standard. The glossy black is in drop D, and the blue is drop D and half step down."

After the message was relayed, the tech asked about the last guitar. He quickly replied to the tech, "I'm going on with this one, but it'll be half step down."

The girl with the clipboard was still yelling at him as Lila watched the tech call in another hand to help with the guitars.

He tried his best to calm her down, "Tiff, calm down. I've never missed a show," he said in a soothing voice. "Lila this is Tiffany, Tiffany this is Lila," he announced as he introduced them.

"Oh I see. Is this the reason why you're late?" Tiffany said as she glared at Lila while aggressively tapping her pen on her clipboard. They were very aware that Tiffany was not calming down anytime soon.

Joe and Thompson came around the corner. Joe carried his drumsticks twirling them in his fingers. Lila noted that Joe was much taller than either of his friends, well over six feet, and a very broad built man. Even though his stature was larger than life, Joe was every bit of a gentle giant. He had one of the warmest and most compassionate hearts his friends had ever known. His black Red Hot Chili Peppers shirt was a perfect match to the tattoo on his arm peeking out of his sleeve. Joe's short clean-cut dark hair helped to disguise his incredible drumming talent in everyday life.

Thompson had a bass guitar strapped to his back. His dirty blonde hair fell just short of covering his eyes. Thompson had a much skinnier composer, but in no means scrawny. The black t-shirt that he wore bore no logo while hiding his beautiful personality. It was a mystery that would soon be solved, which in his own way, was uniquely complicated.

"About fuckin' time dude!" Joe exclaimed before giving him a fist bump.

They laughed and joked for a minute about how he had 'cut that one close'. Then he introduced both of them to Lila. She could barely get out the words to say that it was nice to meet them.

Lila was still paralyzed with shock as the pieces to the puzzle were slowly falling in place. She could not do anything but watch as he pulled out a red electric guitar, slung it over his shoulder, and started checking the tuning. She realized it was the guitar from the train, but this was the first time actually seeing it. He finally looked up and saw the horrified look on Lila's face.

"Why didn't you tell me?" Lila begged while he stayed focused on the guitar until the task was complete.

He could hear the other band wrapping up their set. "I didn't mean to upset you. I wanted it to be a surprise," he said with concern in his eyes as he tried to explain while slinging the guitar around his shoulder.

Lila eased up a little, "I'm not mad, I'm very surprised. Very shocked and surprised." She calmed down and he pulled her close to his body, the guitar was now resting on his back. "So this is it, this is what you've been hiding all day?" she laughed as it was all making sense now. Lila played back the day in her head as she analyzed his calm and cool composure. Now it was all making sense she thought, the way he was treated so highly by everyone around him, how he knew and got along with everyone he came in contact with, how smooth he was, even when he thought no one was watching.

Looking down into her eyes he replied, "Yeah, I didn't want to tell you because I was nervous that you wouldn't like me for me. For who I am." He could hear that the band was done and the announcer would be calling them on in just a moment.

"So, you're like a rock star or something?" she asked.

"Yeah," he laughed. "I'm like a rock star or something."

He leaned in and kissed her. A big long kiss like they had the first time. The world fell away. Nothing else mattered. There was no stage. There was no audience. Just them alone in their own world, one where they never wanted to leave.

Finally, he pressed his forehead against hers. Their noses almost touching and said, "I gotta go be a rock star and shit." He turned and walked away as they announced the band onstage. Without looking back, he walked right out into the lights of the stage. The guitar glimmered across his back as he raised his hands towards the audience and the crowd let out a powerful roar of excitement.

Tiffany walked over to Lila. "Come on," she said, as if it were an inconvenience. "You can stand with me right here by the curtain."

Lila walked over to the edge of the curtain that was just off to the side of the stage. From here she could see the full band and the crowd. The size of the building was impressive. There must have been three hundred screaming fans packed like sardines into this room. She could hear him strumming his guitar the same way he had while sitting on the back of the car earlier in the day. But now, each chord was an explosive of sound bursting into the audience. She watched his every move as he found his way to the microphone on stage. He let out a screaming warm welcome into the microphone and the audience replied with deafening loud cheers. Lila was as captivated as the audience. She watched as the drums came alive under Joe's hands, as if a freight train was crashing through the stage. Lila's body pulsed to the beat as Thompson strummed his bass. Lila focused on the guitar as it screamed out in distortion. She realized that she had never heard him really sing before. Other than in the car, she thought, but never him alone, and that was just a whisper at that. A snarling scream built up in his throat and exploded through the microphone launching into the audience followed by a deep and tender voice. Lila stared, trying to comprehend the beautiful and delicate scene before her.

Tiffany broke Lila's incapacitated gaze, "You act like you've never heard them play before."

Lila, still in awe, "I haven't really," she replied without her sight leaving the stage.

"What?" How have you not heard them play?" Tiffany asked in confusion, staring at the awe struck girl beside her.

Lila looked at Tiffany with childish shy eyes, "I met him this morning on the train. I had no idea until a few minutes ago that he was even in a band."

Tiffany's face lit up with excitement and amazement. "Are you serious? You didn't know who Layne Michael was before today? You didn't know he was the lead singer of the band, Bad Habits? Oh my god, that's so funny!" she exclaimed.

Lila had only known his name, but had no idea of any significance behind it. She looked back at him on stage watching his golden blonde hair as if it glowed in the spotlights. She noted to herself how his flannel hung effortlessly from his shoulders down to his ripped jeans. As he pounded away on the guitar, Lila could feel the vibrations in her chest.

"I thought you were just some groupie he had picked up," Tiffany announced as she loosened the scowl towards Lila. "But now that I think about it, he's never brought a girl with him to a show."

"Really? Why?" Lila asked her curiously. She still felt that there was so much more to learn about him.

Tiffany pondered for a moment, "I don't really know. I've heard that it was something with his ex-girlfriend. He never talks about it though; it's all just rumors. Girls try all the time to get his attention, but very few ever do."

Lila tried to remember what the girls had said earlier about his ex-girlfriend, but the afternoon had become a blur.

"You're really lucky, he's an amazing guy," Tiffany added with a hint of jealousy.

Lila smiled back at her, "Yeah he is."

Just then, a shadow came walking out of the backstage room behind them. Lila turned to see Katelyn's familiar face. As she approached them, Katelyn took off one of the two lanyards she wore around her neck and handed it to Lila. Lila studied it in her hands as she looked over the backstage pass fixed to the end of the lanyard.

"Layne wanted me to come get you and take you into the crowd," Katelyn announced.

Lila, still in a confused state of shock, asked, "Why didn't any of you say anything about this earlier?"

Katelyn laughed as she replied, "He asked us not to. He said he wanted to surprise you."

Katelyn grabbed Lila's hand and guided her around the curtain to a dark door. Once through the door, Lila was greeting by blinding white lights and as she regained her focus, Lila saw a security guard next to a rope that separated them from the crowd. She stood before hundreds of people bouncing and full of energy. The melodic wave of their bodies ripped and curled from wall to wall like a magnificent ocean. Katelyn pointed towards the front of the crowd near the stage and the security nodded his head as he unlatched the rope. She dragged Lila through the crowd, weaseling her way to the front of the stage. The people, who were running in a circle, pushing, and shoving each other as they danced just a few feet away, intrigued Lila. Punk rockers with long hair, mohawks, and all types of bright colored hair dye filled the circle as their black clothing and chains bounced around in unison. Katelyn was unfazed as she meticulously fought her way through the crowd. She must have done this a lot, Lila thought to herself.

They finally came to a stop just a few people shy of the stage. Only a few feet separated Lila from the boy she had spent all day with. He seemed different now, she thought, almost larger than life as he stood there on stage before her. A stray light illuminated his body from behind as he stood glowing above her. All of the confusion and shock left her body at once as it was replaced by excitement. Lila let out a huge scream as she started jumping along with the crowd. She felt free and alive as she became one with the music. Her long dark hair leapt and bounced across her shoulders as she shook her head along to the beat. Her body felt weightless as her feet left the ground, as if suspended in zero gravity.

The song came to an end and the crowd clapped and cheered. They had just played three songs back to back and Katelyn and Lila were excited to catch their breath for a moment. Katelyn reached down into her pocket and produced a flask that she quickly took a swig before handing it to Lila. Without hesitation, Lila took a swig of the warm alcohol. With everything that had been happening tonight, she needed a drink. The girls watched and laughed as the band made jokes about each other into their microphones and interacted with the audience. The guitar tech from earlier quickly swapped guitars with Layne, readying him for the next song. Lila was amazed how the crowd was eating up everything they said. She had never witnessed an audience so engaged. The crowd had an energy of it's own and she could feel it inside her. Lila and Katelyn passed the flask back and forth a few times before Katelyn finally put it away. Another song started and the crowd was jumping in unison once more. As the song went on, Lila could feel the alcohol relaxing her body and intensifying her excitement.

As he stood on stage, he had noticed Katelyn and Lila had worked their way through the crowd. The energy from the room filled his entire body as he wailed on his guitar. The louder they played, the more the room reacted. Occasionally, he stole glances at Lila, gauging her reactions to the music. The larger the smile on her face grew, the more confidence built within him. The music was tight tonight. Joe was on fire with a thunderous roar protruding from the back of the stage launching out into the audience. Thompson set the melodic and rhythmic tempo with his smooth bass lines interweaving the drum hits like the beautiful craftsman he was. The electric guitar exploded with an overwhelming heavy distortion that threatened to bring the building down to its foundation. And all this was tied together with Layne's vocal mixture of soft soothing singing and heartbreaking painful screaming. Each chorus was sung by the three hundred-person choir pushing Layne forward from line to line.

On nights like this, he felt as if he was in a dream, a realistically magical dream that he dare not wake up from, for fear of it vanishing in a moment. But it's not a dream, he thought to himself, this is my life, this is what I've always wanted. Standing there on stage in front of all these people, he wore his heart on his sleeve, standing there naked for the world to judge him and in return, they accepted him for who he was. His lyrics tapped into the subconscious mind of anyone who would listen and he was able to put into words what they all thought, but did not know how to express. He was truly one of a kind and his talent reflected this.

The lights from above the stage came down and focused their attention on the drum set. Lila watched patiently as the song came to a dead stop. It was only a matter of seconds, but with the growing tension from the crowd, it felt like an eternity. Joe broke the silence with the bass drum pulsating through the dense air. The toms exploded with every hit of the drumsticks. The drum kit grew larger than life under the lights as the tempo advanced. Soon the splash from the symbols echoed off the walls as the snare sprang into action. The crowd clapped, yelled, and screamed, pushing the solo forward. Lila watched as Joe's hands became a furious blur battling the drums with amazing accuracy. Suddenly the stage lit up again as the bass and guitar filled the air once more finishing the song altogether. The crowd was more than pleased. In the down time between the songs, Thompson jumped on the microphone to keep the energy flowing. Layne took the moment to run a water bottle to Joe and compliment on his showmanship. A tech appeared from backstage carrying the blue electric guitar and quickly swapped out the glossy black guitar. Once switched, Layne quickly made his way back to the microphone.

As the intro riff to the song screamed out of the guitar, Lila recognized it instantly as the song Layne had played on the back of the yacht. Now she realized how everyone else had known the words, it was one of Layne's own songs. Lila was surrounded by the lyrics to a song she had only heard once before as the audience sang out.

"Thank you so much for coming out tonight!" Layne cried over the rumble of the audience. "We hope you had a great time! We can't wait to see you all again!" he added as the last of his guitar feedback screeched through the amps.

The crowd applauded as the three waved their goodbyes and slowly made their way off stage grasping at the final moments as the lights dimmed down. Lila had lost track of how many songs had been played. Her heart was pounding through her chest to the beat of the subconscious rhythm in the room. People all around her were still jumping and hollering in excitement. The intensity level had peaked to eleven and there was no turning back. A chant started from the back of the room and grew momentum as it rushed the stage crashing like a tidal wave. Soon it was clear that they were not ready for the show to be over as they cried out in unison for an encore. Suddenly the lights sprang back on and the three rushed back out onto the stage ready to provide the people with what they wanted. This time Layne carried the guitar that he had bought earlier that day.

"What happened? Did you miss us already?" Layne announced with a laugh and the crowd boomed with a response. "All right, all right! Luckily we have a few cover songs to play you!"

And just like that, they were off again. Thompson's bass guitar shook the crowd with the intro riff to Jet's, "Are You Going To Be My Girl". Layne smiled at Lila as his guitar came screaming in. Lila was star struck as Layne sang directly to her. She wanted to be his girl and she felt it in her heart. After everything she had learned about him throughout the day, Lila felt more and more captivated by him. He had drawn her in like an overwhelming force of gravity that she had no desire to contest.

Katelyn turned to Lila shaking the flask revealing that there was just a little bit left, waking Lila from her trance as the song ended. They each took a swig and finished it off. Both of them were feeling satisfied as the last of the alcohol seeped down into their bodies. For the first time, Lila knew the words to the songs and sang along with everyone else. She felt as if she was moving in slow motion and fast paced all at once. There was so much to focus on all around her that it was almost difficult to process. She watched how Katelyn's necklace bounced off her shirt and stayed suspended in the air in perfect unity with her soft blonde hair before dropping back down to start all over again. The girls laughed and danced and sang to one another in the sea of people around them.

Kate and Katherine pushed their way through the crowd until they finally found Lila and Katelyn. James, Timothy, and Gregory followed behind, panting and sweating.

Lila greeted them with a smile, "Hey! Where were you guys at?" she yelled through the audience.

Kate replied on their behalf as the guys tried to catch their breath. "They were running the whole time in that circle thing," she rolled her eyes sarcastically at James.

Catching his breath for a moment James announced, "It's a circle run, thank you very much! And it happens to be awesome!"

As the song was coming to the end, Layne suddenly let out a death-defying scream throughout the building. The crowd tried their best to hold their own, but it was no match for Layne's power and volume of his voice. As the drums and bass played on, nothing but feedback left the guitar. In a simple swinging motion, he threw the guitar over his head and swung down with nearly enough force to break through the stage. The crowd exploded as shrapnel from the guitar shot through the air. Everyone around Lila burst out in excitement, jumping up and down trying to get a glimpse of the action. She watched through holes in the crowd as Layne violently attacked the stage over and over with his blonde hair flailing around in complete dismay. His muscles tensed and flexed as the guitar was sacrificed piece by piece. The euphoria of the moment captured Lila. Time slowed as the shiny black pieces of the guitar stayed suspended in the air feet away from her. She watched as he released every bit of aggression and pain out on the guitar. Suddenly she had an uncontrollable urge to expel an emotion-fueled scream out of her body. It felt like a twisted knot in her stomach that gained speed and sprang to life right up and out of her.

Layne stood tall on stage with nothing but the neck of the guitar left in his hands. Raising his arms above his head, he casually threw the neck on the ground behind him. Now screams and cheers of content echoed throughout the building as the band said goodbye one last time. Katelyn made a motion with her hand pointing to the door that led backstage. They all followed her through the crowd still reminiscing on the concert. Lila felt so surreal walking through the still screaming crowd. The performance had been electrifying, like nothing she had ever witnessed before. Soon they were in front of the bouncer flashing their backstage badges and waved through the rope to the door before she knew it.

"That has to be the best show yet!" Timothy announced to the group as they walked through the door.

They were all in agreeance as they shared little stories from the night. The group found Layne, Joe, and Thompson relaxing in a makeshift circle of chairs just off the side of the stage. They all congratulated the three on a job well done. Lila walked over and sat on Layne's lap as Joe and Thompson asked her how she liked the show.

"It was amazing!" Lila exclaimed before giving Layne a kiss, unable to express in words how she felt.

"I'm glad you liked it," he responded with a simple smile across his face.

"I can't believe you didn't tell me about any of this," she said with subtle frustration in her voice.

Thompson chimed in to help out, "Trust me, he always has a way of amazing us."

"That's for sure!" Joe added.

"You destroyed your brand new guitar!" Lila stated in confusion. She had noticed that it was the same one he had bought with her in the shop that morning.

Layne did not respond, other than his big-hearted smile.

"He tends to do that during the shows," Joe answered for him while laughing.

Lila could feel that his shirt was soaked with sweat, but it did not bother her. She had witnessed how much of a workout he had gotten on stage.

Layne finally responded to her question. "I told you I get a little passionate when I play and they tend to break," he said in a joking way.

"I would say a little passionate is an understatement," Thompson chimed in.

They all laughed as Lila was at a complete loss for words.

"Where's Nicole at Joe?" Kate asked. "What about Jeff, Thompson?" she added.

"She just left a few minutes ago to pick Sidney up from work," Joe replied. "But they'll be at the party tonight."

"Hell yeah dude! Party at my house like always!" James belted out, still riding his high from the concert.

"For all I know, Jeff is probably still out there dancing," Thompson shrugged as Kate laughed and agreed.

Layne looked up at Lila, "Me, Joe and Thompson have to clean everything up and get it to Thompson's house, so you can ride to the party with the girls if you don't mind."

"That works for me," Lila replied. She turned to Katelyn and asked, "Is that okay with you?"

"Of course that's fine! We have room in our car," Katelyn exclaimed.

Everyone said their goodbyes as Lila kissed Layne and followed the group out the side door.

CHAPTER 7

The summer's night air was crisp and refreshing against the sweat under Lila's shirt. She ran her fingers through her hair as she took in a deep breath of cool air, finally realizing how hot it had become inside. James and Timothy led the way through the alley and onto the sidewalk followed by the pack of girls and Gregory taking up the rear. The street was soon swarming with commotion as people fled this way and that way, crisscrossing under the streetlights. The crowd was still very much alive with excitement as it spilled into the streets. Dancing and singing could be seen and heard in every direction as they navigated the streets to their cars. Timothy and James guided the way as their phones buzzed with text after text about the party as they frantically tried to keep up with the demand. The girls talked amongst themselves about all the cute guys they had seen at the show while Gregory listened and laughed along. After managing to walk the few blocks through the city, the group arrived at the cars. The guys hopped in one and the girls piled into the other.

Kate was in the driver's seat; Katherine took the passenger seat leaving Katelyn and Lila in the back. As the car sped away into the night, Katelyn reached down under a seat and pulled out a bottle of vodka and a warm bottle of Pepsi.

"Shots anyone?" she asked as she took a sip from both bottles and passed them to Lila.

Lila did the same and passed them to Katherine. Katherine took a sip of the vodka and with a look of disgust on her face, tried to choke down some soda before the alcohol could get the best of her.

After successfully keeping the shot down, Katherine turned towards the backseat to ask, "So Lila, what did you think of the show?"

"Oh my god! It was amazing!" she exclaimed. "I can't believe that I've never heard them play before," she added.

"So is that what you expected he would be like?" Kate asked with a grin on her face as all the girls waited for Lila's response.

Lila was still in shock, "No way! If someone had told me that I would be spending all day with some rock star I had just met, I probably wouldn't have believed them." She was still recounting all the events throughout the day and still amazed how it had all unfolded.

"That's probably why he didn't tell you," Katherine laughed. "It was probably just easier to show you."

All the girls laughed and agreed. The bottle was passed around a second time as the girls continued talking about the show. Katherine fidgeted with the radio stations until she found one to her liking and all the girls burst out singing. Katelyn danced around with the vodka bottle and used it as a makeshift karaoke microphone.

A slough of cars already lined the street as they neared James' house. Half the show must be coming to this party, Lila thought. Kate parked in the driveway behind Timothy's car and everyone unloaded from the vehicle. James opened the front door to his house as if they were floodgates. The street came alive as nearly every car on the block revealed partygoers. A river of bodies filled the house as Lila watched every inch of countertop and table filled with bottles of alcohol, pizza, bags of tacos and any other snacks she could imagine. An assembly line of beer made its way to the fridge as it was soon packed full. Song requests rang through the house and soon the party was on, fuelled by music blasting through speakers in the living room.

Layne parked the mustang behind Joe's truck in front of Thompson's house. The bed of the truck was overflowing with musical equipment. Layne met them at the back of the truck as Joe, Thompson and Jeff climbed out. They began to meticulously unload the equipment as they had done many times before. All of them laughed and joked about how crazy the party was going to be as they worked. The amps and drum set were slowly reassembled in the basement of Thompson's house as guitars were placed neatly around them. Pleased with their work, the plans were made to drive to the party. The city was quiet in the middle of the night as the engines fired up and took off down the street.

By this time, everyone knew who Lila was, at least some form of the story at least. The girls, who were jealous of her and all the guys who admired her, treated Lila as royalty. Kate, Katherine, and Katelyn had tried to assure her that the other girls were just jealous because they themselves could not be with Layne. Lila still felt a bit uneasy thinking about how fast paced the day had gone and how all these new experiences were just thrown her way. She could feel the way that some people glanced at her, wondering why she was so special. Everything changed when he walked in the door.

Stillness swept through the house as if the tides were changing. Lila watched as the band walked in. She watched as the crowd treated them like Gods ascending down on a party. An unknown light source appeared to illuminate them as they walked through the door left open from the great flood. A round of applause rumbled through the house as they were greeted with a tray of shots and the party continued. They slowly made their way to the kitchen, shaking hands as they went with Nicole, Sidney, and Jeff in toe. Nicole and Sidney had just met with the band outside the house. Another round was waiting on the kitchen counter, which was quickly consumed and followed by another.

Lila watched him with her loving eyes as he made his way through the party. He carried his genuine smile as he laughed, joked, shook hands, and gave hugs. He interacted with everyone the same way he had earlier that day on the beach. Lila noticed he carried a beer in one hand and accepted a taste from every drink or shot offered. Layne saw Lila standing with the girls in the middle of the living room and waved her over to the kitchen.

"Lila this is Jeff, Nicole and Sidney," Layne said as he placed his hand on her lower back and introduced them. "Jeff is Thompson's boyfriend, Nicole is Joe's girlfriend and Sidney is Nicole's friend."

She shook their hands as Jeff added how nice it was to finally meet her.

"We have heard so much about you!" Jeff stated as he kissed her hand. Lila blushed at the thought of them talking about her. "Don't worry sweetheart, I'm sure when you get to know us you won't be shy," he added with a grin.

Lila laughed, "I'm sorry, it has been quite a busy day."

"I can only imagine," Nicole added. "I've known Joe for years and it's still overwhelming sometimes."

Nicole was a gorgeous tall blonde woman who had met Joe years before in high school and they had been together ever since. She was part of the family and the band before there even was a band. Layne and Thompson had always known that Joe would probably marry her someday and they could not see a better fit for him. She was always fun and exciting and they loved having her around.

"Overwhelming? Psst," Jeff snickered at Nicole. "Drinking and parties and music, what more could you ever ask for? This is absolutely magnificent!" Directing his attention back towards Lila, "You'll have to tell me about your day sometime. I would love to hear all about it." Jeff had only been around for about two years now, but he was no stranger to the group of friends. From the very first day Jeff met everyone, he became a part of them almost instantly. With his eccentric and charismatic personality, it was hard for anyone not to like.

Lila assured him that of course she would tell him all about it. Slices of pizza and tacos were being passed throughout the kitchen and everyone indulged. The alcohol was setting in and everyone was in a giddy and happy mood. Layne had made his way through the living room and was working his way back to the kitchen one person at a time while his heartwarming smile led the way. Finally making his way back to Lila, he embraced her with a kiss.

"I feel like it's been forever since I've gotten to kiss you," he whispered in her ear as he wrapped his arms around her.

"It's been way too long," she replied as she bit her lip and gazed into his eyes. Lila felt safe and comfortable in his arms. Any worries she may have had, all fell away as he held her.

"I personally haven't even gotten to ask. How did you like the show?" he said calmly, eager for her response.

Lila pressed on the tips of her toes, pushing her lips close to his ear and with a sensual whisper replied, "You're pretty amazing, but I think you already know that." With a playful nibble on his ear and a quick kiss on his cheek, she relaxed her poise exposing her big beautiful eyes once more. He could not help but smile at her, as he got lost in her eyes.

Nicole and Jeff had been trying to casually watch their interaction. They had both seen Layne with girls before, but nothing like this. It became very obvious to them that this was something different. They tried to secretly analyze what they were seeing.

"He is absolutely crazy for this girl," Jeff whispered to Nicole as he covered his mouth with his glass.

"It looks like it! But remember, it's only been a day," she secretly replied.

"Do you think they've had sex yet?" Jeff intrigued.

"It's only been a day!" Nicole quietly shrieked, trying her best not to move her lips.

"Well they certainly will tonight! Look at the way they look at each other," Jeff added, content with his observations.

"It's only been a DAY!" Nicole remarked, trying to emphasize the word day without giving obvious eye darts to Jeff.

Without breaking eye contact, Layne added, "You know we can totally hear you."

Lila blushed. She had pretended not to hear them.

Without a second thought, Jeff wrapped his arms around Lila and Layne and whisked them away. "Come on, let's go out by the pool and enjoy the party!" he said as they walked out of the kitchen.

Nicole followed Jeff as he guided Lila and Layne through the living room. Gregory, Thompson and Joe had all been talking in the kitchen and they soon followed as well. Sidney had already gotten lost somewhere in the party. Kate and Katelyn were already outside sitting by the pool when everyone else joined them. Katelyn had found a small mirror in the upstairs bathroom that she was now using to set her lines on. She was focused in her preparations, sure not to get distracted by the group sitting around the small table outside with her.

"Would you be upset if I did some with Katelyn?" Layne asked Lila, curious about her response.

"That's up to you. I don't want any, but you can if you like," she replied sincerely. She was sure by this point there was nothing more that he could do to amaze her.

Katelyn finished her work and hit her line, putting her craftsmanship to the test. The mirror was then passed around to everyone except Lila. When the plate was passed to Layne, he simply passed the drugs to the next in line.

"I thought you were going to do it as well?" Lila whispered to Layne, leaning in close to him.

He replied with a smile, "No, I just wanted to know what you would say."

Soon cigarette smoke filled the air as a sudden relaxation fell over the crowd. Music swept out of the house filling the void in the coked conversations. Jeff rolled a joint and passed it around the circle. As they drank and smoked, the biggest question on everyone's mind was about Lila and how she liked the concert.

"Okay, well I'm sure you all know by now that when I met Layne I had no idea he was in a band, and it wasn't until we walked backstage into the concert that I finally figured it out," Lila stated.

"Wait! What?" Jeff questioned. "He really didn't tell you until you got there?" Jeff and Nicole were shocked that everyone else knew.

"Yes!" Lila stressed. "I had no idea all day!"

"Oh my gosh! That's priceless!" Jeff let out with a roar of laughter.

Katelyn chimed in, "You gotta admit, that is kind of funny." As she joined in with Jeff's joke.

Thompson burst out laughing as well, "Wait, wait, wait! He didn't even tell you that we were headlining the concert tonight? He just acted like you guys were going to see someone else?"

Lila tried to plead her case, "No! He didn't even tell me we were going to a concert tonight."

Joe was completely dumbfounded by what he was hearing, "Dude! You didn't tell her anything at all?" Without waiting for a response, Joe turned to Lila and added, "And you just got in a car with him, someone you had never met, going somewhere you didn't know, and just trusted him?" He was nearly speechless by this point, "What if he was a kidnapper or something?"

The thought had never really crossed her mind and she felt incredibly embarrassed. Her face began turning bright red as Layne tried his best to save her.

"It wasn't completely like that," Layne stated in a childish voice.

"It was kind of like that," Kate finally added.

Everyone laughed and joked at how crazy the story seemed to be. Layne held Lila's hand trying to comfort her, but could not hold back the sheepish silly grin on his face.

Joe finally spoke up trying to comfort her as well, "We are just messing with you, but you have to admit, that is a crazy story."

They all had their fun jabbing at the idea of Layne being a kidnapper. Katelyn passed around her bottle of vodka for everyone to take a shot when someone noticed that James, Timothy and Katherine had been missing for a while.

"Hey where's-."

Suddenly Timothy came bursting through the sliding glass door leading to the pool in nothing but his underwear. James was quickly behind him with his pants off and trying to wrestle his shirt as he ran. Katherine quickly followed James and was already in her bra and panties as all three made a dash for the pool. Without saying a word, Layne jumped out of his chair and ran into the living room.

"Oh boy, it's about to be one of those parties," Katelyn exclaimed.

Confused, Lila asked, "What is he doing?"

"You'll see," Joe laughed. "He's doing what he does best."

Lila looked at Thompson hoping for a better explanation.

Seeing her concern he added, "Layne likes to take situations that are amazing and throw them over the edge and make them, well for the lack of a better word, spectacular, I guess you could say."

Before Lila could think about it, the song coming from the living room stopped and was replaced by Nelly, "Hot In Herre". Suddenly, people were flying through the door headed for the pool. Articles of clothing were being thrown everywhere. Lila watched in excitement as guys and girls proceeded to strip down completely as they ran to the pool. Everyone started singing along as some girls stopped at the edge of the pool to start dancing to the song while completely naked, glistening in the refracted pool lights. Layne came casually walking out of the house with a huge smirk across his face. Without saying a word he walked up to his group of friends, finished his beer in one large gulp and started taking his shirt off.

"Anyone joining in?" he asked as he stripped down to his underwear.

"When in Rome," Joe replied and quickly followed suit.

And with that they all decided to join the festivities. Lila was slightly hesitant at first, but decided that this day had been strange enough, might as well end it with more excitement. She watched as clothing all around her were thrown to the floor without any care as to where they landed. Layne was already in his boxers and made a huge splash as he cannonballed into the pool. She carefully took her shirt off and placed it delicately on the chair she had sat on. Next came her shoes and socks in a neat little pile by the leg of the chair. By this time, half of the group was already in the pool with the others close behind. Her pants took longer to take off, careful not to turn them inside out, as one leg at a time was set free.

Chanting started from the pool to try and help Lila. "Take it off! Take it off!" was said over and over.

Layne laughed as he watched her, he knew she did not care for the added pressure. Luckily by now, it seemed to not faze her as she simply folded her jeans and set them neatly on top of her shirt. Wearing her bra, panties, and a smile, she calmly walked to the edge of the pool and dove in. Cheers from all around greeted Lila as the party continued.

Sidney walked out of the house carrying bottles of rum and whiskey. She stood alongside the pool, egging the swimmers to take shots as she poured the bottles straight into their mouths. Her snappy personality and short hair made Sidney a force to be recon with. Sidney's part time job as a bartender allowed her to manipulate drunks with ease as she flaunted her talents across the deck of the pool.

Alcohol pulsed through Layne's veins with a calming natural effect. Years of drinking had cultivated an above average tolerance. Never admiring this feat as a talent, like others saw it, he deemed this as just another of his abilities. He would describe the feeling as hitting a plateau, rarely blacking out, and even more rare was vomiting from alcohol, no matter what volume he ingested. Now he calmly swam in a pool filled with chaos, as peacefully as ever. His friends all surrounded him laughing, yelling and splashing as all the cares in the world were whisked away. He realized that in this moment, he felt absolutely no pain. He was amidst an extraordinary moment of perfection. It made him happy that Lila felt so comfortable with his friends. He watched as she seamlessly interacted with everyone she encountered. Layne smiled to himself as Lila and Kate were coerced into taking shots from Sidney. Sidney stood above the pool as the powerful woman she was, gently pouring alcohol into Kate's awaiting mouth. Without hesitation, Lila followed, welcoming the sweet alcohol as it cascaded passed her lips into her yearning mouth. By this time, Layne knew that she could easily hold her own. His friends had fully accepted her into the group without any hesitation, but then again, they would stand behind him in any situation. His friends followed his decisions without question. It was nights like this that reassured their full trust and respect for him, because of course, without him, none of this would have happened.

Lila wrinkled her face in distaste. "Wow! That's a little rough," she exclaimed.

Sidney burst into laughter as she replied, "Yeah, it's not exactly top shelf rum." As she lifted the rum into the light to analyze the bottle, she noticed some tequila had been left on the deck of the pool. "Layne! Come take a shot of tequila!" Sidney demanded.

Layne casually swam between Lila and Kate to the edge of the pool. "Normally I would say tequila makes my clothes fall off, but it looks like any alcohol seems to do the trick."

The girls giggled as they watched Layne pull himself out of the water onto the deck of the pool, flipping his body around to face them. As he sat with his feet still in the water and body on the deck of the pool with his hands bracing the ground at his sides, Sidney grabbed under his chin and forced his head back. Kate and Lila watched as the water dripped from his wet hair and beaded down his chest. The girls stared intently as Sidney stood powerful above Layne guiding the tequila down his throat as she held his head in place while his eyes were locked on hers. Finished with the shot, Sidney released Layne's head, allowing him to return his gaze back to Lila and Kate.

With a smile and an unfazed expression he stated, "That's some good tequila!" as he effortlessly slid back into the pool. Quickly, he grabbed Lila and lifted her body out of the water while kissing her, completely catching her off guard. She put up little resistance as she kissed him back.

As Lila was placed back down into the pool she quipped, "You think you're so cool don't you".

Unable to come up with a quick remark Layne replied, "Duh, what do you think?" as he stuck his tongue out at her.

The excitement in the pool had started to die down as Kate asked Sidney to retrieve towels from inside the house. The night air had grown much cooler now, just on the edge of being a chill. The alcohol was very helpful in keeping people warm, so some decided to stay in the pool for a while longer as others climbed out in search of warmth. Joe, Thompson and Jeff stood alongside the pool wrapped in towels as cigarette smoke billowed out in a cloud above their heads. Katelyn retrieved her mirror to continue her operation in the living room of the house. Nicole and Gregory sorted through the pile of clothing left between the chairs. James, Timothy and Katherine made a dash for the house, following a trail of shirts and pants, to find where their clothes had been left. Layne was able to find his pants, but his shirt evaded him. Lila quickly found his shirt, pointing out that it was right where he left it. She then carefully dried herself off before redressing.

Layne was ready for another beer, so they made their way back through the house to the kitchen. Lila then realized how exhausted she had become from the long adventurous day. Instead of a beer, she asked for a glass of ice water that Layne soon produced. Leaning against the kitchen counter, Lila watched as Katelyn crafted her lines of cocaine now on the coffee table as others gathered around, patiently waiting. She wondered how they could possibly manage to continue doing drugs and drinking without ever slowing down. All of these people around her were so different from anyone she had ever known. They were so carefree and happy while piling mass quantities of substances into their bodies without ever thinking twice.

Nicole had joined them in the kitchen by this time and was asking Layne about when he would be back for the summer.

"My finals will end in two weeks," he replied. "So I'll either be home that Friday night or sometime Saturday. I'm not really sure yet, but I'll be home all summer."

Nicole was fixing herself a drink as she continued her questions. "Any plans for a summer job? Or are you going to party all summer?" Nicole laughed, as she already knew the answer to her question.

"If they keep paying us like this every weekend for shows then I probably won't need a summer job," Layne answered as they clang their glasses together in a cheers. "As long as we keep getting gigs that is. Oh, and we can play Tuesdays and Thursdays throughout the summer. That way we can play almost all week long."

Layne noticed that Lila was fading from the party and realized she had to be exhausted from the long day.

"I'm sure you're going to be fine Layne, keep writing those songs because that set tonight was amazing," Nicole tried to tell him before she lost his attention to Lila.

Layne put his arms around Lila, pulling himself close to her. "Are you getting tired Lila?" he asked her as he noticed her eyes getting heavy.

"Yeah a little," she replied. "It's been a long day." The exhaustion set in as she thought about it.

Layne smiled as he thought of where she could sleep for the night. "Come with me, I'll get you to bed."

Lila finished her glass of water and followed him out of the kitchen. Nicole said goodnight to Lila as she passed. Layne led her up the stairs to the second floor. Layne pointed out James' room, which was the master bedroom, as they passed the door in the hall. The second bedroom was Timothy's, which was a bit smaller and the third bedroom was always left empty for any extra party guests who needed a place to stay. Lila followed him in as he ran and jumped on the bed. She closed the door as she walked over to sit on the edge of the bed near him.

"You better not be expecting to have sex with me on the first day we meet," Lila stated her intentions clearly.

Layne laughed as he replied, "No, I'll let you get some rest. I was going to say goodnight and head back down to the party for a bit," trying his best to reassure her of his good intentions.

Lila relaxed enough to lie down next to him. "Good, because I'm not that type of girl."

"I didn't expect you to be," Layne replied with his loving eyes.

Lila thought for a moment before asking, "Tell something about yourself?"

"Like what?" he replied trying to think of an answer for her.

"Well, how did you learn how to play guitar?" she asked.

Layne caressed her hand with his fingers as he began the story. "It was a long time ago, in a galaxy far, far away," she laughed as he said it. "I really wanted to play an instrument when I was younger. Finally when I was around twelve or thirteen, I took guitar lessons for about a year, maybe two. I can't really remember how long."

"That's it?" she asked in amazement. "That's all you had lessons for?"

"Yeah, but then there were years of practice on my own. It's taken a lot of time and dedication to feel comfortable enough to play in front of people," he stressed.

Lila enjoyed the way Layne moved his fingers in patterns down her arm as if he were drawing elaborate works of art upon her. "What about singing? Have you sang all your life?" she asked.

"No way," he laughed. "We actually started the band before I started singing."

"How does that work?" Lila asked, confused.

"In high school we started out just getting together to jam, just as something fun to do and as we started coming up with songs we decided we needed a singer to add to the band as well. I had already started writing lyrics to the songs that we all liked so we actually had a few different singers, friends of friends and things like that, come in to audition. But since I had written the songs, I had an idea of how I wanted them to be sung. All these people that came and sang with us were amazing, but it just didn't quite fit how it sounded in my head."

Intrigued by the story, Lila wanted more, "So when did you start singing?"

"Well, whenever I would drive around by myself, I would always be singing along to the radio, like most people do, but one day I was really frustrated with some stuff going on, I can't really remember exactly what it was, I started screaming the songs as harsh and as loud as I could. To relieve some stress, I drove through the country by myself with music blaring and screaming to every song that I could. I had expected to lose my voice from doing that, but somehow I didn't. It was kind of weird really."

Layne shuffled the pillow under his head to get more comfortable. "So for the next few weeks I went out in the country over and over doing the same thing. Then one day, after we had auditioned the fourth or fifth singer, we all sat around talking about adding him to the band. Joe and Thompson had really liked him, but I still didn't feel like the songs sounded right. By this time they were getting frustrated thinking I would never decide on anyone. They wanted to go with the last one because they both agreed that he had sounded the best out of the rest. Me being stubborn, I didn't want to give in quite yet and said we should keep looking. Finally Joe got frustrated and asked how the song was supposed to sound since I always said that it didn't sound quite right. So, I picked up my guitar and said I'd show them."

Lila was amazed by the story. "That's how it happened? You just got upset with each other and you started singing?"

"Yeah basically," Layne laughed as he recalled the moment. "They were upset with me and I told them to play the song, so Thompson grabbed his bass, Joe got behind the drums and we started playing. Do you remember the song we played tonight in the middle of the set, the one with the soft verses and the chorus that I was screaming?" He calming sang the chorus to refresh her memory.

"Yes!" she blurted out. "That was amazing!" she added in excitement.

"Yeah, that's the one I sang for them. After we got through the chorus that very first time, Joe and Thompson just stopped and looked at each other. I was still just trying to express how it should sound. It hadn't crossed my mind to be the singer. They just sat there in silence for a moment before finally looking at each other and saying they found the singer. I didn't know what they were talking about at first. I really didn't think I could sing or anything."

Lila was hanging on his every word. She lay there patiently watching his soft delicate eyes begging for more.

"So they finally tell me that I should be the singer, and I'm thinking no way is that happening, but they aren't letting up. Thompson finally calls Jeff downstairs because we were in Thompson's basement and said we had to play the song for him. So we play the song completely for Jeff as he's sitting there on this old crappy couch off to the side of the room. The song ends and Thompson asks him what he thinks. He just sat there in silence for a moment, and I really thought he was going to cry at one point. I'm thinking oh great, my voice really is that terrible. Then all of a sudden he starts saying how amazing it was and how much emotion was in my voice and all that stuff. At that point I didn't know what to think, I wasn't a singer, I didn't plan on becoming a singer. It was all way too crazy for me."

"How did you not know? Your voice is so amazing, I couldn't imagine you not using your talent," Lila stressed.

"I'm glad you like it," he said with a smile.

"I absolutely love it!" she exclaimed. "There's times when your voice is so sweet and soft and delicate that it's absolutely beautiful. Then all of a sudden your voice just explodes with power like you're singing directly for your soul. It's truly amazing." She was full of excitement while trying her best to explain how it made her feel.

"I should probably let you get some rest," he said as he kissed her on the forehead. "It's pretty late."

She was now wide-awake wishing that she could learn anything and everything about him. "Why don't you stay a little bit longer?" Lila said in a low seductive voice with more of a statement than a question.

"So what about you?" He asked as he lay beside her. "What got you into photography?"

Lila thought for a moment. "I think it all started when I was really little and would visit my grandparents," she reminisced in the memories. "My grandfather was a photographer for a local magazine in the Bay Area. He would travel all around with the journalists and take pictures along the way. I loved hearing all of his wonderful stories of his adventures. His true passion though was wildlife photography, so when he was younger, my grandmother and him would go on weekend camping trips deep into the mountains so he could photograph rare and hard to find animals. I loved looking at the thousands of pictures of birds he had in his collection." Her eyes began to really light up. "Oh, and my favorite was when he would teach me how to process the photographs in the dark room. When I was little, it was like magic watching the pictures come to life." A huge smile formed across her face as she spoke. "That's why I was so excited to see that camera today because it's just like one he had in his collection."

Layne studied her excitement and could help but smile as he witnessed her so full of passion.

"You know," she said as she paused her story. "We could share the bed tonight if you want to sleep here as well."

Without giving him a chance to respond she leaned over and kissed him. He went right along with her plan as he caressed the back of her neck with his hands. She emerged herself fully into the moment. She thought about how attracted she was to him and how badly her body yearned to be close to his. Layne could not get enough of her as he kissed her with more passion than he ever had before. His hand slowly worked its way down her back to the small of her waist and pulled her in close.

She whispered into his ear, "You better not sleep with me and then leave me in the morning."

Working his head back just enough to breathe, he replied, "I promise I'll still like you in the morning."

Able to catch her breathe again, Lila only wanted more as her toes curled with excitement. The rhythm of their heartbeats were in sync as her body rocked forward and back. All of her senses were electrified as he pulled her close for a kiss. This is it, he thought, this is the girl I want to be with.

CHAPTER 8

Lila woke with the early morning light shining through the cracks of the window shade. Her body ached as she moved under the sheets of the bed. She soon found herself in a hungover haze as she wondered why she was naked in an unknown bed. The memories of the night slowly came back to her as she remembered where her clothes were left. She painstakingly reached over the edge of the bed to retrieve her articles of clothing as she realized Layne's were missing. Once fully dressed, she found her phone in her pocket and checked the time. 8 o'clock in the morning she read, as the light from the screen blinded her eyes. She had a few missed calls from Stacy and one from her mother as well. After a few quick texts, letting everyone know she was fine, Lila stumbled her way to the bathroom, then down the hall and to the stairs. As she came down the stairs, she could see the partiers fast asleep all across the floor of the living room. Watching her steps, she carefully made her way through the living room to the sliding glass door that led to the pool. As Lila passed the couch, she noticed Katherine was lying on top of Gregory, and they were both in their underwear from the night before. Lila could see Layne through the window before she reached the door.

Layne sat in the early morning sun glancing out over the pool. His glasses pulled tight over his eyes as they shone bright with the reflecting of the sun. His head was glowing with his perfectly messy blonde hair. Smoke from a cigarette billowed into the morning air. A cup of coffee was clenched tightly in his hand as Lila walked to him.

"Good morning Lila," Layne greeted her as she sat down next to him. "I was trying to let you sleep in, I hope I didn't wake you when I got up."

Trying her best to adjust her eyes to the bright morning sun, she replied, "No, I just woke up." Sensing a chilling in air she started to shiver.

Noticing that she was cold, Layne quickly took off his flannel. "Here, you can have my jacket," he said as he offered it to her.

Lila wrapped herself in his big flowing jacket. "Thank you so much, I didn't realize how cold it was out here." Her head started throbbing as she tried her best to shield her eyes.

Layne laughed as he noticed, "Here, take my sunglasses."

He handed over his sunglasses and insisted that she take them. "Would you like some coffee?"

"Yes please," Lila responded quickly as she pulled the shades on tight to protect her eyes.

They shared the cup of coffee as he finished his cigarette. She reminisced on memories of the party and the concert, giggling and laughing at all the silly events that took place. She added how much she enjoyed being with Layne's friends. Lila felt comfortable and at home with them. Layne admired her beauty as she glistened in the rays of light. Her hair seemed just as perfect as when she fell asleep in his arms the night before. Her gorgeous long legs were pulled tight under the shelter of the flannel.

"Any plans for today?" Lila asked eagerly.

"So far I think the only thing planned is a band practice at Thompsons and we have another show tonight," Layne replied, happy to see Lila's smile. "Of course you're invited."

Lila already knew she was invited, she just wanted to hear him say it. "That sounds great!" Lila exclaimed as she quickly covered a yawn.

"There should be plenty of time to rest before the show tonight," he added, as he was worried she was still tired from the day before.

"Yeah, I'll probably take a nap later today," Lila said as she kind of hoped it would be an easier day than the last. Suddenly an idea popped into her head. "Would it be ok if I invite Stacy to the show tonight? I'm sure she would love it!" she added, eager for his response.

"Yeah! That would be awesome!" Layne answered quickly without a second thought. "I can get a backstage pass as well if she wants one."

"That would be amazing! She'll have so much fun!" Lila cheerfully replied as she kissed him on the cheek.

"I saw Katherine and Gregory sleeping together on the couch in their underwear," Lila giggled. "What do you think happened to everyone last night?"

Laughing, Layne replied, "Yeah, I saw that too. They tend to hook up from time to time. They always claim that they are just friends, but it seems to happen a lot. I'm guessing that Thompson and Jeff went home, and Joe and Nicole probably did as well. I'm assuming that Tim and James made it to their rooms last night because I didn't see them anywhere in the living room, but I don't know where Kate and Katelyn are. They could have gone home, but for some reason I have a feeling that they stayed with Tim and James last night."

"Do the girls usually hook up with them?" Lila asked, trying to understand the logistics.

"I think they do from time to time, but it's a casual thing. None of them have ever officially dated." Layne laughed as he thought about the scenario.

Layne thought about the day ahead of them. "I was thinking that we could grab some breakfast and head to my house to get cleaned up before the band practice. How does that sound?"

"Yes!" Lila replied. "A nice long shower sounds great!" Her head was starting to pound from the hangover. She understood now why Layne had worn the glasses so religiously the day before. Any stray sunlight that found its way to her eyes sent a piercing pain through her brain. The glasses were the only shield against the sun.

"What sounds good for breakfast?" Layne asked, as he tried to think of what to have.

"I don't know, but I'm starving." Lila replied while her hand rubbed her stomach.

They debated on where to eat while the cigarette and coffee were finished. The sun provided just enough warmth through the chilling morning air to allow Lila and Layne to enjoy the morning for a few minutes. Layne pointed out all of the empty cups and bottles of alcohol that littered the pool's edge as they reminisced of memories from the night before. When they were finally ready to leave, and breakfast was decided on, the pair made their way through the living room infested with sleeping bodies and out the front door of the house.

Cars still lined the street as they exited the house. Layne pointed in the direction of his mustang as they crossed the front lawn. Lila was careful to keep the sunglasses pulled tight to her face. Her body swayed subtly from her aching muscles as she walked. The memories from the hours of jumping during the concert flashed through her mind as they neared the car. Knowing the drill by now, Lila opened the passenger door without waiting for Layne to unlock it and climbed down inside. As she stretched her legs out across the floorboard, her foot grazed an unfamiliar object. Confused, Lila reached down to find out what it was. She realized what the item was as she pulled it from under the dash.

"Hey! I left my camera in here!" Lila exclaimed, as she looked it over in her hands.

Layne had not realized that the camera was left in the car. "We must have forgotten it when you fell asleep after the boat trip."

"Looks like we'll have to take more pictures today!" Lila added as she smiled at Layne.

Layne was nearly lost in her smile when he realized he should start the car. The engine let out a violent roar as it sprang forward ten feet and died. Layne felt ashamed.

"What happened?" questioned Lila.

With a pout across his face he replied, "I didn't let it warm up."

He tried the key only for the engine to whine, but not start. Taking a moment, and a deep breath, he tried again. The engine fired up in the cold brisk morning and they were ready to go.

As they sped down the street, Layne fumbled between the stick shift and the radio. Lila noticed his early morning struggle and offered to take over the radio controls for him. Since she had studied how Layne worked the old radio, Lila knew exactly how to operate the piece of equipment just like the mad scientist Layne was. She scanned through the Sunday morning commercials hoping to find some music. Suddenly, the opening to "She's Electric" by Oasis caught her attention. They both looked at each other in excitement as they began singing along to the song.

Layne's window was down with his arm resting on the window seal as his hand gracefully caught the morning air. Lila seemed alive and full of energy as she sat with her legs curled in the seat towards his body. Her sweet soft voice was harmonizing an octave higher than his deep voice and filled the car with a wonderfully warm sound. Her beautiful singing mesmerized Layne as they raced through the empty city.

They had decided on a quick fast food breakfast as the mustang pulled into a parking lot to enter a drive-thru. The music was halted momentarily as the food was ordered and received. Before pulling out of the parking lot, Layne stopped the car at a gas station next to the restaurant.

"I'm going to run in real quick, do you want anything?" Layne asked as he started to climb out of the car.

Lila thought for a moment before she replied. "No, I'm okay. What are you getting?" she wondered.

Layne looked back with a cheesy smile across his face. "You'll see," he said as he walked towards the gas station.

Lila started to wonder what it would be when her hunger took over and she dug into the bag of food. After a few minutes, Layne came back to the car to find Lila half way through her burger.

"You sure were hungry!" Layne joked as he climbed back in.

"Yeah, yeah. What did you get?" Lila asked, careful not to talk with her mouth full as she studied the small bag in his hands.

"I got something for you," Layne replied with a smile as he pulled a brand new pair of sunglasses from the bag and presented them to Lila.

"Awesome! They are just like yours!" Lila said excitedly as Layne peeled the stickers off and handed them to her. She quickly removed his sunglasses and gave them back as she fashioned her new sunglasses onto her face. "How do I look?" Lila asked, tilting her head towards his.

"Like a million bucks, baby," Layne replied, as his glasses were pulled tight over his eyes. "Now we are ready to roll in style." And with that, they were off again on their journey.

Once back at Layne's house, he quickly found Lila a towel for her shower and made himself at home on his own bed with his breakfast spread out around him. Lila admired his bedroom once more as she noticed new pictures and writings hidden without the art on the walls. She asked questions about some of them while Layne did his best to devour his food and answer at the same time. Lila marveled at Layne's sketches that hung around the room, which consisted of realistic drawings of trees, plants, flowers and birds. She was amazed with the amount of detail and effort he had put into his sketches. In between taking bites of his breakfast, Layne told her about how he would listen to records and draw while he pointed to the record player hidden in the corner of the room.

Lila walked over to the record player as she asked, "Do you still have some records? I would love to hear one."

"Yeah!" Layne burst out quickly. "I have to dig through my closet to find them, but I can get some out for you."

"I would love that," She added, as she gazed over the record player. Realizing he was almost done with his breakfast, Lila knelt down beside her luggage that had been left in his room from the day before. "I'll take a shower while you find some records," she said while digging through her clothes.

"Sounds good to me!" Layne replied with a smile.

Lila picked out an outfit for the day and with a towel over her shoulder, gave Layne a kiss before she walked down the hall to the bathroom. Layne finished his breakfast and opened the closet to where he thought the records should be. After quickly moving a few things around, he uncovered a tub of records and pulled them from their hiding place. After dragging the tub to the center of the room, he sat down and began flipping through his collection. Memories rushed through his head as he flipped through the records. It had been a long time since he had listened to them, but he could still hear each and every song playing as he saw the albums. He remembered the days when he would go to thrift stores and sift through the old records to find the hidden treasures nearly lost in the stacks, then running home, anxious to hear the records he had found. He remembered the blissful feeling in anticipation of the needle drop from which the songs would be unlocked and how he would sit and draw for hours listening to album after album, as he grew deeper and deeper into the music. Those were the days of complete carefree living. Long before the days of the band, long before he wrote his own songs, long before heartbreak. Unplagued by teenage angst, he would sit in his room, surrounded by art, listening and creating.

An album broke his daydream as he admired the simple cover. A bird's skull sat in the middle of a blue background. Layne smiled as he remembered the day he had gotten the record out of his father's collection. He carefully pulled the record from its sheath and placed it on the record player. The speakers let out a scratching hiss as he cleared the dust build up from the needle. The shower stopped as he heard Lila moving around in the bathroom. He knew she would be able to hear the song as he followed the grooves of the record to the ninth song and dropped the needle right as his selected song began to play. Lila recognized the song as "Peaceful Easy Feeling" by the Eagles as she got dressed and walked down the hall while the music grew louder and louder as well as the smile on her face.

"I love this song!" Lila said as she saw Layne sitting on the floor with a bin full of records. She quickly hung the towel on a hook behind the door that was being used to dry her hair and joined him on the floor.

They laughed and joked about the albums he had, as she requested songs for him to play. As each song ended, she was ready with another and he would systematically operate the record player for her. Lila impressed him with her knowledge of the artists he kept in his collection. She sat across from him, holding the albums she deemed silly and questioned his judgment. His face gave out a slightly embarrassed childish look as he pleaded his case. Lila continued teasing him just to see his reaction.

"Abba is awesome! I don't care what anyone says," Layne exclaimed in his defense.

Lila giggled as she looked over the album cover. "Yeah, I like Abba too, but I never expected you to have it."

"What's that supposed to mean? I'm only allowed to listen to punk rock since that's what my band plays?" Layne joked as he snickered at her. He was now pulling clothes out of his closet and readying a towel for a shower.

"I guess you're allowed to like them," Lila said with a cheesy smile as she set the album down and continued her search while Layne walked down the hall to the bathroom.

By the time Layne's shower was done, he was dressed and ready for the day with another pair of torn jeans and a black Foo Fighters t-shirt. He could hear The Doors album playing through the house. Entering the bedroom, Layne found Lila lying across his bed with one of his sketchbooks opened as she glanced through. He noted the way she was fixated on his drawings, sometimes tracing the lines with her finger as she looked over the sketches. He admired her long legs as they flowed across the bed with her jeans clenching tightly to them. The nearly see-through white shirt she wore almost revealed the outline of the black bra she wore underneath.

"I found some more of your drawings, I hope you don't mind," Lila stated with innocence in her voice.

Layne replied as he took a seat next to her on the bed, "No, I don't mind. Did you find any you like?"

"Yes! All of these are amazing!" Lila said as she flipped through the pages.

Laughing Layne replied, "I don't know about all of them. They are mostly just quick sketches."

Layne's phone started ringing as he pulled it from his pocket and quickly answered the call. Lila could tell that Joe was on the other end, but could not hear much of the conversation. She continued to study Layne's artwork. After the call was over, Layne told Lila that Joe was stuck at home and could not find his keys.

Layne was confused as he tried to relay the message to Lila, "Joe's all upset that he can't find his keys and something about toothpicks being everywhere."

"Toothpicks?" Lila questioned. "What about toothpicks?" She was just as confused as him.

"I have no idea," Layne chuckled. "Joe's house is just around the corner, we could go help him out."

Lila agreed that they should help Joe and the two of them quickly cleaned the pile of records that had been left on the floor. Layne grabbed a flannel jacket from the few that were hanging in the closet and slipped it on. Lila asked if she could continue wearing Layne's flannel from earlier. He was pleased with the question as he watched her drape the flannel over her delicate body. Soon they were out of the house and back to the car, eager to find out what was happening with Joe. Lila was amazed that Joe really did live around the corner as the mustang parked behind Joe's truck outside of his house. Lila noticed a gated courtyard that led to the front door of the house as Layne explained to her that Joe had to come unlock it for them.

"Joe!" Layne cried out. "Come unlock the gate."

Suddenly, a bedroom window flew open as Joe's voice came booming out. "I can't unlock the gate because I can't find my keys!" Joe said in a panic. "And there's toothpicks everywhere!" Joe added.

Layne and Lila stared at each other confused. "How are we supposed to get in?" Layne finally shouted back at the window. "And what toothpicks are you talking about?" he questioned as he laughed and smiled at Lila.

"The toothpicks, they're everywhere," Joe was still shouting through the window. "I can open the garage for you guys."

Within a few moments the garage door slowly opened. Layne led the way through the garage. Lila admired a sliver drum set that sat in the middle of the garage. She noticed that it was different from the set she saw the night before. Layne explained that it was Joe's practice kit. Lila followed Layne into the house through a living room, passed a kitchen, and into a second living room that led towards a bedroom. Lila could already see Joe in a frantic and confused state as they entered the ransacked room. Toothpicks and miscellaneous items were sprawled out across the floor while Joe leaned against a nightstand staring down at the mess.

Layne burst out in laughter. "You're right Joe, there are toothpicks everywhere!" Layne and Lila tried carefully to not step on them as they stood in the room.

Joe was still frantic, "I got home last night, used my keys to get in the house, put them on this nightstand and then went to bed, and now I can't find them anywhere! And this damn box of toothpicks fell over and exploded when I moved everything off the dresser and nightstand looking for the keys!" Joe quickly shifted his tone to a calm demeanor, "Good morning Lila."

Lila was caught off guard with the scene in front of her and began to laugh as well. "Good morning Joe."

"Did you have fun at the party last night?" Joe calmly asked.

"Yes I did!" Lila quickly replied.

"That's good," Joe added peacefully before turning his anger back to the toothpicks. "These fucking toothpicks are everywhere!" he boomed. "I have no idea where those fucking keys are, I've searched everywhere. I even looked through the house thinking maybe I set them down before I got to my room."

Layne was laughing so hard that he could not catch his breath long enough to reply. He just stood and watched as Joe picked the entire nightstand up and moved it over revealing the hidden location of the keys. Layne's eyes started watering as he pointed and laughed hysterically at the keys sitting on the floor. Lila felt so bad for Joe that she tried her best to cover her mouth in hopes of not letting her laughter escape.

Joe let out a roar as he leaned down to retrieve the keys, "What the fuck!" Joe studied them in his hands as if they were something magical. "Well, are you ready to go jam?" he asked as Layne tried his best to pull himself together.

Layne was still wiping the tears out of his eyes when he replied, "Yeah Joe, let's get out of here. We'll help you clean this up."

Handfuls of toothpicks were gathered and returned to their original box. Notepads, a jar of change, pocket knife and a lamp were all set back onto the nightstand and soon the floor was clean again. Joe ran around the house turning off lights and shutting windows as they prepared to leave, and then led the group out of the house. Crossing the courtyard, Joe said that he was going to stop for breakfast and he would meet them at Thompsons. Goodbyes were said and the cars took off down the street.

CHAPTER 9

The mustang flew across town with ease on the quiet Sunday morning. The city was still waking up and there were barely any cars on the road. Layne pointed towards a giant white house on the corner of a busy street as he told Lila that it was Thompson's. She was amazed at the size of the house as the car pulled off the road. An old oak tree had an obvious bend in the trunk, as it seemed to sit on the front porch. Layne explained that the tree had fallen over onto the porch many years before and continued growing, giving it the unique appearance. Lila was still in awe of the house as they exited the car. This time, she made a point to not forget her camera as she fashioned the sling around her neck and let the camera hang down to her side. She quickly followed Layne through a gate and to a side door that he knew would be unlocked.

Layne did not slow down as he entered the house. "They are probably still sleeping," he said as he quickly made his way up the stairs to Thompson's bedroom.

Lila removed her sunglasses in the same fashion as Layne as she followed behind him. She noticed the unusual set of stairs, which split into two, one way leading down into another room and the other leading to the second floor of the house. Reaching the top of the stairs, Layne found the bedroom door closed and gently knocked on the door. Waiting for a response, Layne told Lila about how he would climb out onto the roof to bang on the bedroom window when they were unable to wake up. Thompson shouted through the door letting them know that he was awake and he would soon accompany them in the basement. Layne then led Lila down the stairs, this time taking the new set where it split into two. Lila realized now that it led to the kitchen as they walked through another door leading to the backyard.

"This house is a maze," Lila exclaimed as they walked through the backyard towards the basement.

"Yeah it is. They'll be excited to give you a tour of the whole place," Layne replied with a smile as he opened the basement doors, revealing a dark set of stairs.

The soft cool touch of the basement air embraced Lila as she followed Layne down the stairs. He weaseled his way along a short winding path of boxes and old broken chairs. A single naked light bulb illuminated the direction in which they headed. Lila looked around Layne's shoulder wondering what could lie before them. Through the darkness, she could barely make out the far walls of the basement. Lila's eyes were slowly adjusting from the change of light to dark. The musical equipment came into view as Layne and Lila rounded a water heater. Joe's drum set was against a brick wall facing the center of the room, while the bass and guitar amps faced each other on either side of the drums. A small amp attached to a microphone was placed in front of the kick drum, while half of the guitars were leaning against amps and the other half were off to the side, laying across a table. Layne stared at the selection of guitars before choosing his red electric. Taking a seat on a stool near his guitar amp, he began to tune the guitar. Lila found her way to an antique couch that faced the equipment. She was noticeably startled when the entire couch shifted and rocked as she sat down.

"Sorry, I forgot to warn you about that," Layne told Lila. "It has a bad leg on it, but it wont fall over." He said with his big bright smile.

"Thanks for the warning, I thought my heart was going to stop," Lila said with slight sarcasm.

"Oh, it's not that bad," Layne replied with a smirk.

Lila readied her camera as Layne prepared his amplifiers. She quickly snapped a candid shot of Layne with his guitar slung over his shoulder, with one hand on the neck of the guitar and the other reaching out for the amplifier knobs. He then made his way to the microphone amplifier and on his way back to his seat, he dragged the microphone stand closer.

Layne strummed his guitar and adjusted the volume to a quiet reasonable sound. "Would you like to hear a song?"

"Of course!" Lila replied, patiently waiting with her camera for a perfect moment.

He strummed his guitar as the sound of the chords elegantly filled the air. The basement had its own natural echo, adding a peaceful calming feel to the music. He began singing in his soft sweet demeanor as his voice danced around the room. A lone window, high above the drum set, showed a single beam of sunlight as it illuminated his body, while everything else around him disappeared into the darkness. Lila recognized the Bob Dylan song immediately. She snapped a picture as he crouched his head over the microphone while smiling at her. In this moment, He was singing to her and no one else. She could hear the full depth of his voice without the hundreds of screaming fans. Lila loved every moment of it as she lost herself deep into the song. Her heartbeat synced to the rhythm of the guitar. Her eyes caressed over his body as she relived the feelings from the night before. She was lost in his world and she loved it.

As the song ended, Lila reached for a guitar placed on the table next to the couch and slowly admired it as she ran her fingers across the strings.

Noticing the moment Layne asked, "Can I see your camera real quick?"

"Sure," Lila replied as she handed the camera over to him before quickly moving her attention back to the guitar. "Will you teach me how to play sometime? I've always wanted to learn a full song."

"Of course I will. That would be fun," Layne added as he quickly snapped a picture of Lila with his guitar.

Lila heard the click of the camera and quickly asked, "Are you taking pictures of me?" Her playful shy tone was obvious to Layne by now.

"Maybe," he answered with a chuckle as he handed the camera back.

Lila carefully placed the camera back in its bag and set the guitar back on the table.

Thompson, Joe and Jeff were in mid conversation as they bumbled down the basement stairs. Joe found his seat behind the drum set while Thompson stopped at his bass amplifier. Jeff flopped himself down on the couch alongside Lila, sending tremors through the broken couch.

Jeff already had half a beer in his hand when he said, "Good morning Lila. How was your night last night?"

"It was great!" Lila answered. "That was a really fun party!"

Jeff smiled, "I'm glad you had fun. We are so excited that you are here with us today."

"Thank you Jeff, it's been such an amazing weekend. I'm so glad that I've gotten to meet all of you," Lila said thankfully.

Jeff smiled and took a sip of his beer, "And just wait for tonight because it starts all over again."

Lila stared at the beer bottle with disgust in her eyes. "How can you possibly be drinking already? I feel so hung over that a beer would make me sick."

"You get used to it, and once you start drinking again, the hangover is gone," Jeff said cheerfully.

"Damn right!" Joe added from behind the drums.

Jeff was curious to ask, "So? Did anything happen with you two last night?"

Lila started to blush, as she knew what he was asking.

Layne quickly came to her defense. "We were pretty tired, so we went to bed early," he said confidently, hoping his answer would suffice.

Joe remarked sarcastically, "Right, went to sleep."

"Of course you did," Jeff said as he winked at Lila, causing her embarrassment to ease.

Layne chimed in again, "Alright, let's play some music."

The amplifiers rang out with the aggressively heavy guitar as the drums followed quickly behind the bass. The room was alive with a new feel now. The sweet and soft tones Layne was playing just minutes before were replaced with the exciting and fast paced riffs, booming from the speakers. The couch vibrated with the bass guitar under Lila, as she felt a part of the music. Jeff waved and danced with his beer in his hand along to the melody. Lila watched with excitement as the three commanded their instruments.

After a few songs, Jeff leaned over towards Lila, "I'm going to have a smoke outside. Would you like to take a break with me?"

"Sure," Lila replied as the amplifiers rang in her head.

Outside, Lila followed Jeff to a wooden table in the backyard. He quickly climbed over the bench and sat on the table. Lila sat down beside him, careful to make sure the sunlight was blocked from her face. Jeff reached over to a small ice chest in the middle of the table and grabbed another beer as he finished his first. After setting the beer bottle beside him, Jeff reached in and grabbed a second one.

"Here, try it, it'll make you feel better," Jeff said as he offered the beer to Lila, while noticing her hangover.

Lila took the bottle and studied it in her hands. "I don't think it's a great idea." She thought about it for a moment then took a sip. "Oh that's horrible," she exclaimed as she tried to force it down.

Jeff started laughing, "After the first beer you'll feel great." He watched her as she set the beer down on the table. "You know," Jeff started as he pulled a cigarette from his pack. "I don't think I've ever seen Layne as happy as he was last night with you." He lit the cigarette as he continued, "I mean, don't get me wrong, he's a happy person. He loves everyone and everyone loves him, but there was something more to it last night. It was something about the way he looked at you that was different than I've seen before."

Lila was trying her best to interpret where the conversation was leading. "Do you really think he likes me?" she asked worryingly. "I know this is all happening so fast, but there's something different about him. I've never fallen for someone so quickly, or possibly this hard before," she added quickly.

"Oh, I know he likes you," Jeff replied with a grin. "You can see it in his eyes. I've seen him around many girls before, but I've never seen him like this," Jeff added as he gave Lila a wink.

"But what about the other girls he's dated? I'm sure he had to have cared about some of them," she tried to justify.

Jeff puffed on his cigarette, deep in his thoughts. "You know, I've never seen him really date anyone. There have been a few girls who have hung around longer than the others, but I think most of the time it scares him that they are attracted to him just because of the band." Jeff was trying to choose his words carefully.

"Yesterday Kate, Katherine and Katelyn mentioned something about a girlfriend he had a long time ago. What about her?" Lila was weary to ask.

Jeff thought for a moment about how to begin this conversation, "I wasn't around when Layne was dating her. I met Thompson just a little while after they had broken up, so I've only heard the stories from everyone else. Layne rarely talks about her, and even when he does, he never says her name. I think I've heard him say her name out loud probably twice at most in the last few years."

"I probably shouldn't ask," Lila started to say before the rest of the words fell short.

"No it's ok, Layne's a pretty open person, he just doesn't care to talk about her all that much, but really who would want to talk about an ex," Jeff laughed as he ashed out his cigarette and grabbed the beer bottle. "Here's what I've gathered from the stories," Jeff said as he took a sip from his beer. "They fell in love with each other very quickly. Layne was head over heels for her and everyone could see it. Of course this was when they were young and in high school, but his friends did think that it would last a lot longer than some high school fling. Apparently, once they were together, they were inseparable. If you invited one, you invited both without having to ask. And they were never like some couples, which cut themselves off from the rest of the world. They each had their friends, but they brought them all together. Layne's never been the person to leave anyone out. He's always been a great guy. They would spend all day, everyday together, as if they just couldn't get enough of each other. When they were apart, her friends would say all she ever wanted to talk about was how amazing he was and how much in love with him she was. So anyways, I'm a little fuzzy on the details exactly of why she broke up with him the first time, but it shocked everyone, including Layne of course."

Lila took a sip of her beer, patiently waiting for the story to unfold. Music was still flowing through the basement door loud enough for her to feel the crash from the cymbals.

Jeff continued, "So one day, just kind of out of nowhere, she breaks up with him. Says something like, 'She just can't do it anymore', but she would never fully tell him why, and then that unfolds into months of getting back together only for her to break up with him again and again. Thompson said that it was so consistent, you could set your watch to it. Every few days she would apologize and want to be together again, then break up with him and kind of disappear for a bit, only to come back and start all over. Layne was so helplessly in love with her that he did everything he could to be with her. That's how she was able to continually break his heart over and over. After they graduated, she finally broke up with him for the last time and he was devastated. She cut herself off from everyone, not just him, but her friends as well. Within a few weeks she changed her number and moved away."

"Oh my god, that's horrible." Lila added.

"Yeah, for awhile it pretty much destroyed him. That's around the time that I first met Layne. Of course he was always funny and kind to me, but there were times where you could almost see this darkness in him. It's hard to explain. Anyway, months would go by and he would hear rumors of where she was, but no way to get ahold of her."

"Is that when he started partying and getting a little wild?" Lila asked, trying to fit the pieces to the puzzle.

Jeff laughed, "A little wild might be an understatement. Layne was drinking heavily. He was going out to parties as much as he could. He would out drink anyone. Do more drugs than anyone. Act wild and crazy, but always the life of the party. That's where his stories started to turn more into legends. Everyone wanted to party and be around him. It wasn't a real party until Layne was there. He was so good at talking to girls, that he could talk to a group of girls and set them up with his friends without them having to do anything."

"Oh geez," Lila laughed as she took another sip of her beer.

"Sorry," Jeff apologized. "I was trying not to go down that road."

"It's okay," Lila assured him. "So what else happened?" she asked eagerly. The beer was starting to go down easier and her body was slowly feeling better.

"So, during this time, he seemed so happy to the outside world, but really he was dying on the inside and doing anything he could to escape the pain. So Layne thought of a way to get the girl back. He wanted to do something for her he was sure she would love. Over the next year, he wrote and recorded an entire acoustic album using a cheap microphone and his laptop. He worked for countless hours secretly by himself. He could already play the guitar by this time, but he was practicing for hours a day just on the guitar. That's when he also started to develop his beautiful voice while he was practicing alone. Back then he had no intentions of becoming a rock star or anything like that, he was just trying to win the heart of the girl he loved."

Lila was intrigued, "So what happened, did he find her and give her the songs?"

"Well, not only did he write these songs for her, but he kept this notebook as well. He filled the notebook, cover to cover, with poems, stories, lyrics and drawings. Anything he could think of that reminded him of her, anything that he could think of to bring her back. So after an entire year, he was finally finished with his project, but he still didn't have a way to get ahold of her, so he set the notebook, with the album in it, hidden away at the top of his closet and there it sat. As the weeks turned into months, his hope was slowly fading away. After another year without hearing from her, he was sure that he might never get his chance."

Lila finished her beer and set it down silently on the table as Jeff went on.

"One night, she calls her friend and tells her that she's driving into town and wants to see Layne. Her friend quickly relays the message to him and half an hour later, she's at his house. Now they haven't seen each other in over two years, let alone talked, so it had to be horribly awkward for him."

Lila quietly signaled for another beer while trying to not interrupt the story. Jeff fetched another bottle from the ice chest as he lit another cigarette.

"He had said that she was just as beautiful as the day she left. He didn't know what to say other than the usually small talk, so he gave her the notebook and told her there was a CD inside for her to listen too. She promised that she would listen to it and she left. The next few days were torture for him. He frantically worried about what she would think of everything. She finally calls him so they go meet up. Layne was nervous, excited and scared. He had no idea what to think, he just wants to know if she liked the songs, the poems, the drawings, the stories. He's so nervous when he sees her that he just blurts it out."

Jeff took a long drag of his cigarette and drank from his beer.

Lila waited patiently for Jeff to finish, but he just sat in silence. "Well, what did she say?" Lila finally asked.

"She said that it was 'a pathetic cry for help' and that she could only listen to a few songs before she turned the CD off," Jeff finally added.

"What?" Lila confusingly stated. "But after everything? After all that work, all that time and energy, she just says that to him?" She sat there in shock.

"Yeah, he was devastated. After that, she left again without a trace and he fell into a deep depression. He tried to drink away his pain, but this time it just didn't work. He told Thompson one night that he was never going back down that road again, and he would do whatever he could to end it. We were all worried, but there was really nothing we could do. He hid away from everyone, drinking alone. When you would see him, he just wasn't quite the same anymore. I don't like to say this, but there were a few times where I seriously thought we were going to lose him." Jeff finished with a sigh.

Lila sat in silence. She did not know what to say. She could hear Layne's voice slicing through the instruments as the music overflowed into the backyard. Lila could now understand how he could relay his pain through his voice. It was more real to her than ever.

Jeff waited a moment for Lila to take it all in. "Can I ask you something Lila?"

"Sure, what is it?" she replied confused.

"Well, have you ever thought about why Layne would take the train to and from Fresno?" he asked.

Lila thought for a moment, not knowing where the question was leading. "No," she responded. "What do you mean?"

Puffing on his cigarette he clarified, "I mean, Layne has a car and Fresno is only about two hours away so why doesn't he just drive? He's really only saving a few bucks by taking the train and he ends up not having a car to get around the city once he's there."

The thought had not yet crossed her mind as she sat perplexed with the newly proposed situation. "Why does he take the train then?"

Jeff smiled as he grasped the beer in his hand. "Here's my theory. I think he connects with the train."

"How so?" Lila asked intrigued.

"He sees the train as a metaphor for life. Once he's on the train, he's trapped and at the mercy of where it will take him. When he's inside, he can't see straight ahead, only where he's at in the moment out the windows. Of course he knows where he's going, but he doesn't technically know how he will get there without being able to see the tracks in front of him. The stops along the way are a form of his memories where he's able to get out and enjoy life before it takes him to his next destination. In his own unique way, it's how Layne stays in control after everything he's been through. That's where I think you come into the story Lila."

"What do you mean?" she asked.

Jeff continued as he sipped on his beer, "Layne's on a path to greatness. Anyone can see it. But what they can't see is how much it scares him and that's where you come in."

Lila listened intently.

"He needs someone to guide him, to show him the way, someone that can reach into his soul and extract his excellence and his talents. I've seen the way he looks at you, you bring out something magical in him. It's like an energy that needs to be harnessed."

"So you're saying I should be his guide?" Lila laughed at the comment.

"Don't just be his guide, be his train." Jeff smiled back as the alcohol soothed his body.

Lila pondered the statement for a few moments while they sat in the morning day sun. She tried to wrap her head around what Jeff was saying before wanting to know the end of the story.

"So how did he get through it? That must have been so tough on him," Lila asked.

"One day something just kind of clicked. He got Thompson and Joe together and showed them some songs that he had just written. Some of the songs he played last night were from that first day he showed them." Jeff said excitedly as he raised his beer for another sip.

"Let me guess!" Lila blurted out. "That's when they decided to form a band?"

"That's exactly what happened!" Jeff answered. "Within a week, Joe moved his drums down into the basement along with Layne's amps and guitars. They even went and bought a bass guitar for Thompson to play. I don't know if you know this, but Thompson is exceptional at piano. He learned how to play bass for the band." Jeff stated proudly.

"That's amazing! I would love to hear him play sometime!" Lila exclaimed.

"I'm sure you will," Replied Jeff. "There's seven pianos and organs throughout the house. I can give you a tour of the house later!"

Lila sipped on her beer. "I would love that!"

Jeff continued his story, "When they first started practicing, Layne wasn't singing yet, no one knew he could sing, not even him. That girl had broken his spirit so badly that he didn't even want to try."

Lila listened intently to Jeff's version of the story.

"In the beginning, Layne was writing the music and the lyrics but wanted to bring in a singer to join the band. They auditioned a few really good singers over the course of a few weeks, but Layne kept saying he had a specific sound in his head and no one seemed to be quite right. I would always sit down in the basement and listen to them practice and I thought that a few of them were amazing, but luckily Layne was right. The band wouldn't have been the same if someone else were singing. So one day, after the last singer had left, Thompson, Joe and Layne started arguing about who should join the band to sing. I ended up going into the kitchen to make some food when a few minutes later, Thompson comes running in telling me I have to go down to the basement right away. Thinking nothing of it, I go down and sit on the couch when they start playing a song and all of a sudden, Layne's beautiful voice comes bellowing out of his body. I'm pretty sure I had a few tears running down my face as I realized, we all realized, he was definitely going to be the singer."

Lila chimed in as Jeff told his story, "Yeah! And he told me last night that you guys had to convince him that he was a great singer because he didn't even believe it at first."

"Yes!" Jeff exclaimed. "It actually took us awhile to convince him to sing," He added with a laugh.

"That's absolutely amazing." Lila stated with a smile as she thought about the scenario.

"Once it was decided that he would sing and they started practicing all the time, they were always drinking and trying to play, so you could imagine it was a drunken mess. Luckily that didn't last long. Layne decided that there was no more drinking allowed during practice. He really wanted to take it seriously. They all agreed and things got much better. That's why he never drinks on the day of a show. Thompson and Joe might have a few beers, but nothing heavy and they never ever get drunk before a show because they know how important it is to Layne. Afterwards, all three always celebrate and party."

Lila knew that Layne had not drank the day before. He had said the reason was because he was driving, but now she realized it was because of the show he had not told her about. She noticed the music had stopped as the three came climbing out of the basement.

"Smoke break!" Joe announced as he fumbled through his pockets for a lighter. Jeff grabbed his from the table and handed it to Joe. Layne climbed onto the table next to Lila as she complimented them on their music. Layne thanked her and asked what they had been talking about.

"Oh just you," Jeff replied with his contagious smile as he took a hit from a newly lit cigarette.

"Nothing bad," Lila added, as she kissed him on the cheek.

Thompson suggested that Jeff should start the BBQ soon to prepare for lunch as he inspected the empty beer bottles sitting on the table next to Jeff and Lila. Jeff agreed, as soon he gave Lila a tour of the house. Joe added that he could call Gregory to see if everyone wanted to come over for a BBQ. Layne also suggested that Lila could invite Stacy as well. All the plans for the afternoon were made as they laughed and joked with Lila. Within a day, she had become part of the group.

"Look at it," Joe pointed out. "She's becoming a girl version of Layne!" Everyone glanced at Lila and started laughing. "The flannel jacket, even the same sunglasses!"

Lila tried her best to defend herself, "What? I like these glasses and this jacket is comfy."

Layne rested his hand on her lower back. "It looks very good on you."

Lila thanked him as Joe and Thompson finished their smoke break. The band decided to continue their practice as Layne gave Lila a kiss and the three headed back down to the basement. Jeff ran into the house to grab more beer leaving Lila to call Stacy. She quickly got ahold of Stacy and tried her best to explain how amazing her weekend had been so far.

"There's so much I have to tell you about!" Lila said over the phone.

"So! Is he a nice guy?" Stacy asked.

"He's amazing! And we are going to a concert tonight!" Lila exclaimed.

"A concert?" Stacy said, confused. "What kind of concert?"

"A punk rock concert. I'll explain when you get here," Lila could hardly hold back her excitement as she twirled her hair.

"Okay, okay. It'll take me like an hour or so," Stacy finally agreed.

"Perfect! See you soon!" Lila added as she hung up the phone.

Jeff waltzed out of the house with a graceful stumble. "Are you ready for a tour?" he asked Lila.

"Of course!" she replied as she followed him in through the kitchen.

The small kitchen contained an antique stove and refrigerator. Fine china and crystal glassware filled the cabinets with see-through glass doors. Through a small door sat a breakfast table and an open pantry covering an entire wall. Lila commented on how small the kitchen was and Jeff explained how it was customary at the time the house was made.

"This house was built in 1909, so the service quarters are much smaller than what we are used to today," Jeff assured her.

Through a swinging door, they walked into the formal dining room. The large dining table could easily host a decent size dinner party. The table was set with the finest of silverware as if awaiting guests' arrival. Built in china cabinets were located in the corners of the room, housing old bottles and glasses.

Lila was amazed with the presentation. "This room looks like something you may see in a museum."

"Yes! This entire house is like a giant work of art," Jeff replied with enthusiasm.

Lila followed Jeff through a short hallway that he explained was located under the staircase, and into another small room. An organ with beautiful brass pipes reaching for the ceiling was placed against an entire wall. Across the room were elegant armchairs and a couch under a decorative stained glass window, allowing colorful rays of light to infiltrate the room. Paintings filled the walls all around providing Jeff with plenty of talking points. As Lila listened intently to all of the information Jeff had to offer, she could feel the vibrations of the music being played in the basement. The bass frequencies tore through the house while the thin walls were no match for its power. Jeff led the tour into a longer hallway with the first stop being a room he called the library. Lila gazed in to see bookshelves all around completely filled with books of all sizes. A small reading area was equipped with a couch and a pedestal with an open encyclopedia sitting on top. The end of the hallway opened into a room with a grand piano, a table big enough to be a dining room table, and a magnificent brick fireplace. Over the fireplace, hung a quite large painting of a naked woman praying. Chairs lined the room as if a small crowd could watch a performance from the pianist.

Jeff stopped and marveled at the piano. "This is usually where

Thompson and Layne practice the new songs Layne writes. I've spent many long nights in here watching Layne play his acoustic guitar while Thompson accompanies him on the piano." Jeff pointed towards the empty whiskey bottles left on the table. "That's still left over from their last few writing sessions." He then pointed to a small room adjacent to the room they stood in. "I'm quite sure that this is Layne's favorite room in the whole house. It's usually where we find him sleeping after those long nights." Jeff giggled to himself.

Lila peered into the small doorway. Jeff called it the Turkish Room because a large hookah was set on a coffee table in the center of the room. It was a tight squeeze to fit a couch and chairs around the table. Jeff explained that in the winter, the room stayed toasty warm and was also the coolest in the summer when a slight breeze flowed through the open window. Jeff tried his best to explain the floor plan to Lila. He stated that if they had left the kitchen through another door, that they would have walked into a room with two player pianos. He insisted that they tour the second floor and then they could exit through that room at the end.

In the basement, the practice was winding down. Joe was sitting behind his drums, glancing at pictures in a magazine that had been left behind a few weeks before. Thompson sat on his bass amplifier watching Layne intently as he practiced a new melody with his guitar volume turned down low. Layne was always working on something new in his head and Thompson was always eager to find out where his creative process would lead. Joe was much more relaxed when it came to working on songs. Him and Thompson both had a unique natural gift for creating music, but Joe would wait until the song needed drums and then played what he felt. Within a few moments, he could try out different beats and settle on the one that accompanied the tone for the song.

"So when are you moving back from Fresno for the summer?" Thompson asked.

"Two weeks," Layne replied without looking up from his guitar.

Thompson seemed satisfied with the answer. "Good, what's the plan for moving in? Are you coming straight here? Or moving back home for awhile."

Layne paused his guitar so he could be more attentive to the conversation. "It'll probably be easier to move straight in when I get back. Is that alright with you?" he asked Thompson.

"Yeah!" Thompson said with enthusiasm. "That'll probably be the easiest." He turned his gaze towards Joe. "When are you and Nicole moving in?" he asked.

"Well," Joe thought for a minute. "Since we don't have a show booked for next weekend, then we could move in next Saturday."

Thompson agreed, "That'll be perfect."

"I have finals coming up so I wont be in town at all next weekend," Layne added.

"That's alright," Thompson assured. "I'll be around so I can help you Joe."

"What about Lila?" Joe joked. "Will she be moving in with you as well?" he said with a snicker.

Layne laughed at the suggestion. "I doubt it, that's moving a little fast don't you think?"

Thompson commented with his observation, "At the pace you're already going with this girl, you might as well move in together in two weeks."

"Yeah, yeah, yeah," Layne laughed. "And then what? We'll be married in two months? Absolutely not!"

Joe came to his rescue, "Seriously though, It's about time you found a girl you really like."

"Yeah well, let's just see how it works out," Layne replied modestly.

Lila's body obstructed the light of the doorway to the basement as Layne watched her walk down the stairs. He gazed lovingly as she took the sunglasses from her face and gently secured them in the breast jacket pocket of her flannel without missing a step. He was fascinated and captivated by her elegant walk as she approached him.

Drawn to her eyes, Layne asked, "How was the tour?"

She instantly filled with excitement as she explained how much she enjoyed the house. Thompson asked her what she liked best and gave additional information on the history of the house to further fascinate Lila.

"And the pianos are amazing!" she added. "I would love to hear you play sometime," she stated to Thompson.

"I'm sure that can be arranged," he assured her. "God knows I have enough of them lying around," he joked.

After the conversation, Lila turned her attention back toward Layne. "Is there a phone charger around? I didn't get a chance to charge my phone last night."

"Yeah, I have one in the Turkish Room you can use," he replied and they headed out of the basement and into the house.

Lila acknowledged the artwork as they moved from room to room, showcasing her newly learned knowledge of the paintings. Layne was pleased and listened intently as if he had never heard it before. As they neared the Turkish Room, Lila asked why it was his favorite.

"Because it has the comfiest couch in the whole house," he replied with a cheesy smile.

Lila laughed at his silly and simple response. Layne showed her where he kept the phone charger plugged into an extension cord near the couch. He offered her the couch and suggested that if she wanted to rest before the BBQ that it would be a perfect time. Lila agreed and stated that Stacy always ran late, so it may be awhile before she got there. Layne sat beside her as she lay on the couch.

"Have I gotten to tell you how beautiful you are?" Layne said as he caressed her hair.

Lila's body grew warm with the compliment. "You're quite handsome yourself," she replied in a soft loving tone. Her hand reached for his and caressed him with her delicate fingers. Just being in his presence, she felt calm and at ease. With every touch of his skin, sparks of electricity shot through her body.

Layne laid across her chest, still playing with her hair as she fell asleep. He wanted to spend every moment with her. His feelings for Lila had grown faster than anyone before, and he could not get enough of it. He closed his eyes, listening to the deep melody of her heartbeat, trying his best not to fall asleep. He knew the guests would be arriving soon, and he wanted to lend a hand to the BBQ. Layne carefully forced himself to wake up, easing himself off of Lila, careful not to wake her. He took one last glance and smiled as he left the room.

CHAPTER 10

Lila awoke to the hazy sound of a phone ringing. She felt as if she were waking from a coma and trying to interact with the world for the first time. Finally realizing what the annoying sound was, she reached over the edge of the couch to find her phone. Stacy was on the other end, informing Lila that she had just arrived. Lila's body woke instantly as the thoughts of conversations ran through her head. She told Stacy to park behind the mustang and she would be outside in a moment. Gathering her composure, she quickly traced the rooms of the maze to a side door that led to the street. The warm air greeted her as she stepped out into the sunlight. Carefully placing her sunglasses over her eyes, she met Stacy at the car.

"I'm so glad you made it!" Lila shouted as she gave Stacy a hug.

"I know! I'm so glad to see you! How has it been? What have you been up to? What's he like? What's with this house?" Stacy exploded with questions.

Lila tried her best to hit the highlights of the weekend, "Well, he's amazing. He took me on his friend's boat yesterday afternoon. He's the lead singer of a band and we went to his concert last night, then to this crazy party."

"Wait what?" Stacy was shocked. "He's the lead singer of a band? And he took you to his concert?" she clarified as the information processed in her mind.

"Yes! And he kept it a secret until we got there! It was crazy!" Lila exclaimed as she relived the surprise of the experience while guiding Stacy to the door of the house.

"So are we going to his concert tonight?" Stacy asked as she walked into the dining room.

"Yes!" Lila said with excitement. "And you're going to love it! It was so much fun!" she added as she headed for the kitchen. "Come on, let's go meet everyone."

"Okay," Stacy said, still confused by the whole situation. "What's the story with this house? This is really cool."

Lila had already started to become accustomed to the house. "Oh yeah, I can have Jeff give you a tour of it. This place is amazing."

In the kitchen, Katherine and Sidney worked furiously to prepare the food for a buffet style lunch. The counter was covered with hotdog buns, hamburger buns, potato salad, macaroni salad, regular salad and condiments of every kind. Katherine pulled two Stella Artois from the fridge and offered them to Lila and Stacy as they were introduced. She informed them that lunch was almost ready and everyone was hanging out in the backyard. Lila was welcomed by a sea of faces she recognized as she stepped outside. She realized an entire party had started while she was asleep. Music was being played through the speakers in the basement, seeping out for everyone's enjoyment throughout the backyard. Lila noticed a group of familiar faces as she headed towards Joe, Thompson, Timothy and Nicole standing around the BBQ. They were talking as the smoke seeped out from under the lid of the BBQ, filling the air around them. They each greeted Stacy welcomingly as she was introduced. Lila pointed out that Thompson played bass guitar and Joe played drums. Stacy was impressed by this as she shook their hands. Nicole held a serving platter as Joe removed the BBQ lid to expose an array of hotdogs and hamburgers covering the grill. He quickly dodged the smoke as he pulled the meat from the grill, lining them around the serving tray. Nicole rushed the food into the kitchen as Joe announced that lunch was ready. As people began to file inside for the food, Lila noticed that Layne was sitting on the wooden table with an acoustic guitar in his hand. Katelyn and Kate were on either side of him as he made up silly songs off the top of his head to make them laugh.

"Lila," Katelyn yelled out. "Come join us."

Lila walked toward the table as Stacy followed. Stacy noticed that Layne looked almost identical to the day before with his mirrored sunglasses and flannel jacket. She was still in disbelief that he was the lead singer of a band. The beauty of the girls sitting besides Layne overwhelmed her. Katelyn and Kate quickly made room for the girls around Layne as Stacy was introduced.

"I'm glad you could make it," Layne told Stacy. "I hope you're ready for a crazy night!" he added as the girls around him giggled.

"Yeah! I'm excited, it sounds like Lila had a lot of fun last night," Stacy replied as she sipped on her beer.

"Oh yeah," Katelyn added. "We know how to have a good time." she said with a warm smile. "Let's go get some lunch before everyone eats in all," she joked.

The line was slowly dispersing as the food was served. The rooms of the house were alive with chatter as the guests found anywhere they could to sit for their meal. Old scrolls on the player pianos echoed through the rooms, as the house was alive with excitement. In a cheerful drunken mood, Jeff made his way from guest to guest, reassuring that everyone was accommodated for. He found his way to Lila and was pleased that she was awake from her nap. He excitedly introduced himself to Stacy and told her how lovely it was to meet her. He offered to give her a tour of the house when she was done eating, and she quickly accepted. The group then made their way back outside to the table to enjoy their lunch. Stacy asked how they all knew each other and Katelyn explained that they were friends from high school, with the exception of Jeff and now Lila. As Stacy was brought up to speed on the logistics of the friendships, Layne sat close to Lila, lost in his own world. He absolutely adored her, and even Stacy was quick to notice. Timothy and James joined the table sitting opposite of Katelyn and Kate.

"I brought dessert," Timothy said jokingly as he produced a pipe from his hand.

Stacy watched as Timothy carefully packed the bowl full of marijuana and took the first hit.

"Do you smoke?" Timothy asked while holding in his smoke. "I'm Tim by the way," he added before Stacy could reply.

"No, I'm good," Stacy replied, turning down the offer. "Thank you though. I'm Stacy."

James, Katelyn and Kate passed the pipe around, each taking a turn.

"Lila, you didn't tell me you had a hot friend," James blurted out.

Katelyn was quick to shut him down with a stern look. "James, behave yourself for once and be appropriate," she said quickly.

"Sorry, I was just trying to make conversation," James defended himself.

"She just got here," Katelyn stated. "Be polite," she demanded.

Layne could sense the tension between them. "What happened with you two last night?"

Katelyn sat in silence glaring at James as he laughed at the question. "I don't know," James replied. "What happened with you two last night?" James tried to change the focus to Layne.

Layne was quick to keep the game going. "I don't know," he replied. "Kate, where did you sleep last night?" Quickly bringing her to the center stage.

Kate shot eye darts at Timothy. "I didn't say anything to anyone," he rebutted to her intense stare.

Layne and Lila erupted in laughter, as their assumptions were correct on the events of the night. Stacy was lost in confusion, feeling out of the loop. Jeff walked over to the table to ask how everyone was doing.

"Hey Jeff guess what!" Layne exclaimed, ready to give away everyone's secrets. "Katelyn hooked up with James last night and Kate hooked up with Tim!"

Jeff froze with a wide-open smile on his face as he glanced around the table gauging everyone's reactions. Kate and Katelyn covered their faces with embarrassment while James and Timothy looked away, drinking their beer.

"Oh yeah!" James blurted out. "Lila and Layne hooked up too!" he said as he tried to take the focus away from himself.

Jeff laughed, "Well that was a given," he said with a smile still glowing. "Anyone could have seen that coming from a mile away, but all of you! I am shocked!"

Lila blushed as she grabbed Layne's hand for reassurance. Stacy peeked around Layne to give a wide-eyed look at Lila. "You didn't tell me about that!" she said with a giggle.

"I was going to tell you later," Lila whispered to Stacy.

Jeff quickly asked Katelyn and Kate, "So is this going to be a thing?"

"Absolutely not!" Katelyn stated, staring a James.

"Hey, we are just friends, I didn't expect anything," James blurted out, trying to calm Katelyn.

Katelyn eased her gazed. "Okay good," she said with a smile. "It was fun though, so we'll see."

James blushed for the first time in his life as he sipped his beer trying to hide a smile.

Timothy thought of something to say in order to ease Kate, "Yeah, I've known you for so long, you seem like a sister to me."

"Ewe that's gross!" Kate exclaimed with a distasteful look on her face. "Don't say that."

Everyone laughed at Timothy for his inappropriate comment. Stacy was amazed how open everyone was with each other. She enjoyed listening to their conversations. As everyone finished their lunch, Layne asked Jeff if he had seen Joe.

"Yeah, he's in the kitchen. I can go get him for you," Jeff answered willingly.

"That would be great. Can you tell him to meet us down in the basement? We have to rebuild a guitar for tonight," Layne replied as he stood up from the table. "Katelyn, will you join us as well? You're always the best at it," he asked her. "Come on Lila and Stacy, we'll show you how to rebuild a guitar so I can break it again," he finished with a smile.

Down in the basement, Layne and Katelyn went to work on their makeshift workshop. A card table was placed in front of the couch along with folding chairs around to accommodate everyone. Lila and Stacy sat on the couch while Layne and Katelyn took seats in the folding chairs, leaving one vacant for Joe. Layne found the guitar bag containing the broken guitar from the night before as Katelyn helped to spread the puzzle across the table. Joe made his way into the basement, first stopping at a hidden cache of wood glue, brushes and clamps, before adding them to the workspace. Katelyn plugged her phone into an auxiliary cord protruding from the guitar amp as Blink 182 played quietly in the background.

"You're not doing it right!" A voice boomed through the room.

Everyone turned to see a shadowy figure emerge from a small room in the corner of the basement.

Layne blasted back, "We haven't even started yet!"

The shadowy figure stepped into the light to reveal himself. Lila realized it was the same man that had taken the guitars from Layne at the show the night before.

"Well I know that you're not going to do it right." The man replied with a laugh. "And be careful with the frets this time Katelyn!"

"Don't tell me what to do!" Katelyn smirked.

"That's Lee," Joe told Lila and Stacy. "He lives down here in that room and protects our equipment when we aren't around."

Lee greeted them with a smile, "Yeah, and I do a damn good job at it too."

The girls tried to say hello as he slipped back into his room.

Lila and Stacy watched as Katelyn sorted the small black pieces from the body of the guitar. Layne and Joe worked together to reattach the head to the neck of the guitar. Glue was applied to the exposed ends of the wood on either side and carefully placed back together. Layne held the pieces tight with his hands while Joe meticulously placed small clamps, locking the neck back in place. Katelyn had the focus of a jeweler as she carefully painted glue onto the small pieces of the body and gently laid them into place.

The process captivated Stacy. "How did you break the guitar like that?"

Layne laughed as he worked, "I smashed it last night at the show."

"Yeah! It was amazing!" Lila added, still remembering the excitement of the moment. "Stacy, you should have seen it, the crowd went crazy."

"Why did you break it?" Stacy asked curiously.

Layne smirked as he answered, "I like throwing my voice and breaking guitars."

Confused by the comment, Stacy asked, "Why would you do that?"

"Because it doesn't remind me of anything," Layne replied.

Katelyn and Joe laughed at the reference while the statement flew over Stacy's head.

Feeling bad for Stacy's confusion, Joe lent an explanation, "Layne likes to buy a cheap guitar for the shows so that he can smash them on stage at the end of the show. It gives more of a dramatic ending you could say."

Lila turned towards Stacy. "Yeah, I was with him when he bought it yesterday." She turned her attention back towards Layne. "How many uses can you get out of it before it's too destroyed?" she asked.

"That's a really good question," Layne stated as he helped sort out the small pieces for Katelyn. "Joe what would you say, maybe four to six times or so?"

"I think our record is six," Joe replied as he wiped the excess glue from the neck. "He tends to beat them up pretty badly."

The neck was still separated from the body as both pieces were being worked on. Layne explained that he would screw the neck to the body right before the show, allowing the glue proper time to set.

"It won't have a full twelve hours to set, but it just has to make it through one song, so it should be fine. I'll reattach the neck and body so I can restring it right before we go on."

With the clamps holding the small pieces in place, the guitar was finished for now. Katelyn was thanked and praised for her attention to detail as she looked over her work. Joe finished a beer that he had brought down with him as he suggested they rejoin the party. Layne walked over to the guitar amplifier playing music and turned up the volume so that the music could be heard in the house.

By now, the party had spread throughout the first floor. Guests lingered in the kitchen snacking on the left over food as the group made their way into the house. Katelyn stopped at the refrigerator, grabbing more beer for her and the girls. Jeff found the group in the dining room as they passed through and informed them that Thompson was playing the grand piano in the front room. The music grew louder as they drew closer. Layne quickly took a seat next to Thompson at the piano as classical music filled the room. The rest of the group piled into the packed room, trying to find a place to watch the performance. Layne suggested songs for Thompson to play and he quickly decided on a beautiful rendition of Red Hot Chili Peppers' "Otherside". Layne yelled out for everyone to sing along just before he began singing the first line of the song. The crowd erupted with nostalgia. Others flocked to the room to join in the music as well. Soon, people were packed wall-to-wall singing along.

Stacy was intrigued by the way everyone surrounded Layne. She noticed how he had such a captivating personality that brought everyone together. She leaned in towards Lila, "This is amazing!"

"I know!" Lila yelled back over the crowd. "Just wait till you see him on stage tonight. It's awesome!" she added.

As the song came to an end, requests were yelled throughout the crowd and the music quickly began again. Over and over, this went on as Thompson and Layne played as many songs as they could. Each time, they were accompanied with a room full of voices. The house shook with excitement. Beer bottles clang with celebration. The guests locked in and swayed to the melody of "Wonderwall" as the beautiful tone of the piano echoed through the room. Joe rushed in to sing along before telling Layne and Thompson that they had to leave for sound check. Joe asked the guests for volunteers to help move the equipment as he led a team of workers down to the basement. Layne made his way through the room to where Lila and Stacy stood. He assured Lila that it would only take a few hours and he would have plenty of time to pick them up before the show. The three followed the team downstairs to help with the equipment.

Lee was hard at work putting the finishing touches on the broken guitar. "You had a few clamps in the wrong places and those pickups were horrible, where did you get this pile of junk anyway?"

"It was a hundred bucks down at the pawn shop. I wasn't expecting much." Layne replied as he looked over the new and improved guitar.

"Well I carved out the holes to put in some humbucker pickups that I had lying around." Lee added. "It'll have a way smoother tone than these dollar store ones you must have dug out of the trash."

"Right on Lee!" Layne exclaimed. "Thank you so much!"

Joe chimed in, "Yeah! Thank you Papa Lee!"

Lee stopped what he was doing and shot a glance at Joe, "I'll break you in half if you ever call me that again."

"He loves it when I call him that." Joe whispered to Stacy.

Lee carefully handed the guitar pieces to Layne. "I expect those pickups back in one piece so I can use them again."

Layne laughed, "Don't smash the pickups, got it."

Joe broke down his drum set as he orchestrated where each and every piece should be placed in the truck. An assembly line quickly formed through the backyard and out to the truck on the street. The broken guitar was tucked away into a guitar bag with the clamps still in place, careful not to disrupt them. Within minutes, the truck bed was completely filled with every piece of equipment they owned.

Stacy watched as Lila found Layne standing beside his mustang.

She awed at their interactions as they said their goodbyes. As if an old fashioned movie was playing before her, Stacy studied the way they looked deep into each other's eyes after removing their matching sunglasses.

"Aren't they so cute together?" Katelyn asked, startling Stacy out of her trance.

"I wish someone looked at me the way he looks at her," Stacy sighed with jealousy in her eyes.

"I think we all wish for that, especially if Layne was the one that looked at us that way." Katelyn remarked as she waited for Lila.

They continued watching as Layne and Lila kissed and hugged each other before Layne walked to the truck and climbed in. They all watched as the truck sped off down the road. Lila slowly made her way back to the girls as Katelyn suggested they head back to the party.

James and Timothy were arguing as to which strain they would use to roll a blunt as the girls entered the Turkish Room. Kate and Katherine rolled their eyes from the corner of the room as they passed the hookah hose back and forth. Katelyn called the boys immature as she sat between them on the couch, producing a bag of white substance as she fixed a tray for her lines. Lila and Stacy took a seat next to the girls with the hookah as Gregory walked in the room with beer for everyone.

"Where have you been?" Katherine asked Gregory.

"I've been all over the place," Gregory vaguely replied. "What? Are you trying to keep tabs on me now or something?" he smiled back at her.

"No," Katherine was quick to reply. "I just haven't seen you since we got here."

"If you have to know," Gregory insisted. "I was upstairs in that smoking room hanging out with Jeremy."

Satisfied with his answer, Katherine stopped her questioning of him.

Jeff peeked his head into the room in order to check on everyone.

He had always held himself to being a great host, in which he was. Katelyn offered him a line from the plate in front of her, which he graciously accepted. Lila had grown accustomed to the drugs around her by now, but Stacy was mortified. Just like Lila, Stacy had never witnessed cocaine used in front of her and this was all new to her. She watched intently as the plate was passed around from person to person along with a rolled dollar bill. Gregory connected his phone to a speaker in the corner of the room and began playing Modest Mouse.

James looked over his handy work as he prepared to light the blunt. Smoke billowed from the end as he took the first hit. An idea hit Jeff as he raced out of the room. James passed the blunt to Timothy, holding in the smoke as long as he could before expelling it from his lungs.

"Dude," James thought aloud. "Wouldn't it be cool to put a tiny camera on a blunt and pass it around a party, you know, to see what it sees."

"I've seen something like that before," Timothy told James. "I was at this one party where someone strapped a GoPro to a bong that took a video of everyone hitting it that night," he said as he continued the rotation. "It was pretty cool. Then they edited down the hours of footage to a few minutes of the funny faces people made as they hit the bong."

"That would be awesome!" James added as Jeff entered back into the room with a bottle of vodka in his hand.

"Shots anyone?" Jeff announced to the room as he lined shot glasses on the table.

The group cheered with excitement as they toasted to another wild night. The boys chatted amongst themselves as the girls asked Stacy questions about herself. She in turn, was brought up to speed about how the group of friends all knew each other.

CHAPTER 11

Sound check went as well as expected. Joe could not hear the kick drum or floor tom over the whine of the guitar. Thompson's bass amp kept cutting in and out until the cords were finally switched out. The microphone Layne was singing into had way too much distortion for some unknown reason. All of the equipment was finally prepped and ready for the show after the painstaking levels were finally set.

Tiffany found Layne, Thompson and Joe hanging out backstage as Layne fixed the neck of the broken guitar to the body.

"Hey Tiffany," the three said in unison, barely taking their attention away from the guitar.

"Hey you guys, I'm glad you're all here. I have to talk to you about the lineup tonight," Tiffany said as she glanced down at her clipboard.

"Yeah sure, what's up?" Layne asked without moving his attention from the guitar.

"As you already know, this is the biggest venue you guys have played and there's going to be a lot of people here tonight." Stated Tiffany as she brushed her purple hair over her shoulder.

"Yeah!" They all exclaimed at once.

"Thank you so much again for setting this up for us," added Thompson.

"Thank you so much Tiffany, this is amazing!" added Joe.

"Thank you so much. You're the best!" added Layne.

"Okay so, the opening bands are going to do a shorter set tonight. We are going to try to get you guys on at 7:30 tonight," she stated, waiting for their reply.

"That doesn't seem like too much of a problem, but why? Are they trying to get everyone out earlier tonight?" Joe asked, partially confused.

"Well," Tiffany began to explain as a smile formed across her face. "It's actually going to be a bit longer tonight. We actually had a last minute schedule change because there's a band that wants to do a surprise performance so they'll go on after you."

Layne, Thompson and Joe dropped what they were doing and gave full attention to Tiffany.

"So! Who is it?" Joe asked.

Tiffany paused for a moment as the tension built before finally revealing the band as she added, "But you guys have to keep it a secret because no one knows that they are here tonight."

They each jumped to their feet as they begged Tiffany to meet their idols.

"They should be out on the stage starting their sound check any minute now," Tiffany said as the three ran to the curtains at the side of the stage.

Peering through the small gap in the curtains, afraid to be seen, they watched as their heroes stood on the very stage they were on just minutes before. Completely star struck, they were too nervous to open the curtain anymore. The band played a few cover songs during the sound check in order to conceal their identity if any prying ears happened to be around the concert hall. The three watched intently from their vantage point as Tiffany laughed at the way they gawked over the other band.

After the sound check, the band on stage headed towards the curtain that Layne, Thompson and Joe were standing at. The three quickly ran back to the seats where they were sitting around the broken guitar, trying to act as casual as possible while their hearts raced with excitement. As the band came through the curtain, they found the three sitting around the guitar.

Tiffany quickly introduced each band to one another and added, "This is the band that usually headlines for us here," as she pointed to Layne, Thompson and Joe.

The three quickly stood up and shook hands with the band trying to act as cool as possible.

"What have you guys got going on here?" the guitarist of the famous band asked as he pointed down to the guitar.

"Just putting it back together," Layne replied. "I smashed it during the show last night," he said with his award-winning smile.

"Right on man!" the guitarist replied. "We happen to know a thing or two about that," he added as the rest of the band laughed. "So you guys headline? You must be pretty good. How long have you been together?"

"We've been playing live for about a year now," Layne replied quickly.

"Wow, that's pretty good then, I can't wait to hear you guys play," responded the guitarist.

Layne was so full of excitement he could barely form the words, "Yeah! And we are huge fans of yours! We can't wait to see you guys live!"

"That's awesome!" the guitarist casually claimed. "What are some of the songs that you know all of the words too?"

Layne was thrown off guard by the question, but quickly rattled off a list of songs off the top of his head. The guitarist was impressed and thought for a moment before picking a song out of the list.

"What about that one?" he asked. "We usually play it towards the end of our set, would you guys like to come on stage and sing it with us."

The three were completely speechless and frozen with excitement. Layne took in a deep breath before finally replying, "Yeah! That would be awesome!"

"Right on man, that'll be fun tonight," the guitarist said as everyone shook hands again and went their separate ways.

The three waited until the band was out of sight before releasing their excitement. Layne told Tiffany they had to go as they burst out of the door leading to the alleyway. As they ran to the truck, Thompson told them that he did not know the words to the song.

"Then you better fucking learn it right now!" Joe said as he put the song on repeat for the ride back to Thompson's.

Back at the house, the group had moved from the Turkish Room to the kitchen, snacking on whatever left over food they could find. Lila and Stacy were happily drunk as everyone gathered around listening to James tell crazy stories. Nicole had run to the store an hour before and brought back with her the ingredients for margaritas. The blender in the corner of the room had been running nearly non-stop, providing drinks for everyone.

Layne burst through the door as if a wild animal were chasing him. "You guys won't believe it!" he screamed as he entered the kitchen. "You guys wont fucking believe it!"

Surprised by his actions, everyone stood in silence waiting to hear what they would not believe.

"What is it?" James asked.

"Tonight!" he jumped around in excitement. "There's going to be a secret performance by a famous band!"

The room gasped with excitement, patiently waiting to hear who would perform.

"Who is it?" Timothy asked quickly.

"I can't say who it is because they asked us to keep it a secret, but it's going to be awesome!" Layne stated as he found his way towards Lila. Speaking to the entire room he added, "Call everyone you know! This is going to be big!" Layne grabbed Lila and gave her a heartfelt kiss.

Soon everyone in the house was buzzing with predictions of who it could be. A network of phone calls started inviting everyone to the show. Predictions were being made from every room as Layne,

Thompson and Joe were being questioned over and over about who was performing.

"You boys need to eat something, I'm sure you don't want to miss any of the show tonight," Nicole said as she fixed them some plates.

Lila and Stacy were ecstatic. Stacy thanked Lila once again for inviting her.

"I knew you would have a good time," Lila told her. "This is going to be so exciting!"

Layne had made his way through the house telling everyone as much as he was allowed to about the show. He was still high with excitement as he made his way back into the kitchen.

"What time is it? We should get going, we don't want to miss anything tonight!" Layne said rapidly.

Lila tried her best to calm him, "It's okay sweetheart, it's only 5 o'clock. We have plenty of time. Have something to eat."

"The show starts soon, we should get everyone going," Layne said as he stuffed his mouth with food.

The few drivers sober enough to drive were rounded up and given keys to the biggest cars. Flasks were filled with every kind of alcohol imaginable. Katelyn divvied out the last of the cocaine and everyone was ready to leave. Lila and Stacy jumped in the car with Layne while Joe drove Thompson, Jeff and Nicole. The rest of the party piled into any open car they could find and the caravan started towards the show. As cars were pulling away from the house, Layne realized the mustang would not start.

"What's wrong?" Asked Lila.

"The battery might be dead. I think I may have left the lights on even though I wasn't inside for very long." He replied as the last of the caravan pulled away from the house.

"What do we do?" Worried Stacy.

"It's all good. I'll just push start it!" he exclaimed as he jumped out of the car. "Lila, jump in the driver's seat. Can you pop a clutch?"

Lila shimmied across the stick shift into the driver's seat, "I can try!"

Layne began pushing the heavy car at an incredible slow pace down the street. Once it finally started to gain momentum he yelled, "Now!" as the car jumped and banged to life. As quickly as he could, Layne ran for the passenger door and jumped in before the car got away. "Let's go to the show!"

Lila was able to roll through the first stop sign, the second was not as forgiving as the car came to a jerking halt and stalled. Determined to make it to the show on time, Layne jumped back out and began pushing again. This time when the car sprang to life, he ran alongside the driver door trying his best to give instructions through the window. "Put it in neutral!" he yelled through the glass.

"I can't find it!" Lila yelled back.

Layne was losing steam as the car coasted in first gear down the street. "Just pull it out of gear!" Layne shouted as he began to run out of breath.

Lila tried her best, but accidently put the car in second gear as it took off down the road. Now in full sprint Layne was losing the race. "No! Just push it out of gear," he said as his words trailed off under his breath. He stood panting in the street as he watched the mustang finally come to a stop, engine on, twenty yards from him. "Oh thank God," he mustered to himself. Finally reaching the driver's door, he climbed in as the girls laughed frantically. "It's not funny," he added as he chuckled as well and off to the show they went.

Outside of the building, people lined the block waiting to get in. Lila and Stacy were mesmerized by the crowd forming out front. Electricity was in the air as they slowly drove by. Some of the fans recognized the iconic blue mustang and began cheering as they passed. Soon, the entire crowd was chanting the band's name as Lila and Stacy stared out the windows in amazement. The mustang nearly shook from the roar of the crowd.

"Do they always do this?" Stacy asked as she watched the crowd's reaction.

"Yeah," Layne casually replied. "Whenever I show up early."

The mustang turned into the alley way and parked behind the truck. Joe called out to Layne as soon as he exited the truck, "Dude! This is going to be a great show tonight!"

"Yeah! Let's hope we bring our A game tonight!" he replied as they entered the backstage door.

Tiffany ran to the group as they entered. "I'm glad you're here early tonight," she said as she looked over her glasses at Layne.

"Of course," he replied with a laugh. "I'm not going to miss this night for anything."

Tiffany handed out backstage passes to Lila and Stacy before walking towards Jeff and Nicole, handing them theirs as well. Katelyn soon walked in and received her pass from Tiffany.

"I almost thought you were replaced for a moment," Tiffany joked with Katelyn.

"No," Layne reassured her. "Katelyn's always special," he said with a smile.

"Thank you Layne," Katelyn said as she gave him a hug. "By the way, I have a present for you guys since it's a special night."

Eager to find out what it was, Layne watched as Katelyn pulled a bottle of whiskey from her purse. Excitedly, Layne grabbed Katelyn in a huge embrace and thanked her profusely. Joe and Thompson showed their excitement as well with hugs all around.

"As soon as we are done with our set, meet us back here and we'll take shots before the next band goes on," Layne announced to everyone.

The opening bands came into the room, waiting for their moment on stage. Layne introduced Lila and Stacy to each of them as everyone tried to casually hang out. The topic on everyone's mind was the mystery band as it drew closer to the show.

"Did you hear who's playing tonight?" the lead singer of the first band asked Layne.

"Yeah! Are you excited?" Layne asked, trying his best not to give any details away.

"Dude, I'm freaking out," the lead singer said. "I've never seen them live before. This is awesome!"

"Just remember, it's like any other show, don't get nervous out there," Layne reassured him.

"I know I'm trying. It's just a little nerve racking," the lead singer replied.

They could hear the start of the show as the announcer went onstage to introduce the opening act. Katelyn gathered Lila and Stacy to take them out into the audience. Jeff and Nicole followed as well. Layne wished the lead singer good luck as the band took the stage. He then joined Thompson and Joe around the broken guitar as they removed the clamps. Once inspected, Layne carefully restrung the guitar, trying his best not to apply too much pressure to the weak neck. After a quick test to see if it would hold a tune, Layne was pleased with the work. As Layne held the guitar, the three tried to relax their excitement by predicting how the party would be after the show. The second opening band gathered around as well, joining in the conversation. They had all become good friends after playing shows together and were always invited to the parties. They laughed and joked as the other band brought up highlights from the night before.

Lila, Katelyn and Stacy made their way through the crowd to the front near the stage. Jeff and Nicole lingered towards the middle of the crowd, where there was less chance of being shoved around. The first band played calming reggae music. Soft melodies and smooth vibrations floated over the crowd. Most stood standing and watching as the band played their set, while others swayed in place. Everyone knew that the real excitement was later to come as they conserved their energy. By now, the room was almost completely full with fans. The rumors had gotten around, but no one knew for sure who would be performing later in the night. The girls could hear whispers all around as the crowd quietly talked amongst themselves. Lila heard a familiar voice as she was tapped on the shoulder.

"Hey! We decided to see how it is up here for a change," James yelled out over the speakers, just barely audible enough for Stacy and Katelyn to hear as well.

Timothy, Gregory, Kate and Katherine accompanied him as they formed a small group in front of the stage. They would usually watch the shows from the middle of the room, as it was easier to join in the circle run and not get squished to death.

The first band finished their set as technicians rushed the stage to quickly clear the equipment and prepare for the next band. The crowd dispersed as many fans used this time for a smoke break outside on the street. Katelyn and Gregory took this time to take sips from their flasks and pass them around the group for everyone to enjoy. As soon as the equipment was set and ready, an announcer called out the next band's name and people piled back into the room as the music began. This band was much faster paced; a traditional punk band is how Katelyn described their style of music. The energy level in the room quickly rose. The music was much more aggressive as people pushed and shoved at each other. A pit formed in the center of the room. Luckily, the group was just outside of its boundary. Finally, James and Timothy could not take it anymore. They rushed and joined the pit, slam dancing around, allowing their limbs to flow freely to the music. The girls looked on and giggled at their childish behavior. There were very few pauses between the songs as the guitarist flowed gently from one song to the next. The band was easily able to keep the attention of the crowd and the energy level high.

Backstage, the famous guitarist found Layne, Thompson and Joe waiting for their time on stage. He carried an acoustic guitar and asked if they wanted a run-through of the song they would help perform. Ecstatic with the proposal, they quickly jumped at the opportunity.

Layne came up with an idea on how to sing altogether. "What if you and I go back and forth, line for line, and then we all sing the chorus together?" he asked the guitarist.

"That might actually work out pretty well," the guitarist agreed.

The opening chords to the song started off the practice as the guitarist sang the first line, quickly followed by Layne. They each took turns through the verse until the chorus exploded with a wall of voices.

"That was perfect!" the guitarist exclaimed as the song came to an end. "That's going to be a lot of fun out there."

Basking in the excitement of being around his idol, Layne casually asked, "So what made you guys want to do a secret performance?"

The guitarist chuckled at the question. "The music business can tend to get pretty mundane and lifeless at times, with constant tours and everything scheduled out for you months in advance, you have to keep it new and exciting every once in awhile. We have a new tour coming up soon, this gives us a way to have a little practice before the tour and we get to connect with our fans at the same time. So basically it's a win-win for everyone."

"That's really cool," Joe replied. "What made you want to play here in Stockton?"

"We try to stay as connected to the underground as we can. There's been talk that Stockton has a growing music scene powered by a new band with an original sound, so we are quite excited to hear you guys play." The guitarist stated as he adjusted the acoustic guitar in his hands.

"What?" Layne said in shock. "You've heard about us? How?"

"Oh yeah," The guitarist said with a smile. "Like I said, we stay connected."

The punk band wrapped up their set and the transition between bands began with equipment being rushed on and off the stage.

"Good luck out there," the guitarist added as he shook their hands and walked away with his acoustic guitar.

Out in the crowd, Lila waited patiently with the group. By this time, their flasks were almost empty, and Lila was relaxed in a heavy buzz. They chatted amongst themselves during the quick break between sets. This time however, the crowd who left for a smoke break, quickly filled the room before the music could begin. It was clear that no one wanted to miss any part of the show. Stacy expressed to Lila how exciting the show had already been. She warned Stacy of how wild the show will be once Layne takes the stage.

Once the drums and amplifiers were in place, the lights dimmed down. The crowd erupted with applause in anticipation. Joe and Thompson quietly made their way through the dark to their places on stage. A single beam of light shone on the curtain as Layne emerged strumming his guitar calmly every few seconds. The crowd was ecstatic with cheers. Layne gracefully made his way to the microphone at the center of the stage. He hunkered down in a crouched position as if he were ready to attack at any moment. Thompson's bass began filling in the empty space between Layne's chords. The crowd's reaction grew with overwhelming excitement, ready to burst at any moment. The space between chords shortened as Layne strummed faster. Joe started softly with the snare drum, rising in volume and tempo as he escalated the beat. With a swift motion, Layne engaged the distortion pedal and the first song began thundering through the room. With his powerful screams into the microphone, the crowd instantly reacted by jumping to the beat, forming a pit in the middle of the room. The energy throughout the crowd was at an all time high. Three songs were played back to back without a lull in morale.

Stacy could not believe what she was seeing. The enthusiasm of the crowd captivated her. She was completely engulfed with the ecstasy of the experience while she jumped and screamed along with the rest of the group. Lila and Katelyn laughed hysterically as they jumped and bounced off of one another. Timothy and James immediately disappeared screaming into the pit. Gregory and Katherine were overwhelmingly drawn to the pit as well and soon caved in as they joined the circle run. Kate's energy fed off of Stacy and Lila's excitement. Nicole and Jeff had navigated the crowd during the break to join the rest of the group. They jumped and screamed along to the songs, adding as much as they could to the already ear piercing volume of the crowd.

Between songs, Layne distracted the crowd with jokes as guitars were switched and replaced. His natural charisma was evident in times like these. The crowd clung to every word, watching and waiting patiently for what he may do next. Layne never wanted a dull moment during his shows and he worked hard to keep the energy high. The crowd laughed and yelled, hooped and hollered between songs and quickly they were off again, right back into the excitement. The band was on fire tonight and they knew it. Joe banged out his powerful drums, attacking the audience with sound while Thompson grooved with his deep bass tones. Layne's electric guitar breathed new life as it destroyed any doubt of the band not playing at their best. His power driven vocals were a force to be reckoned with as they pierced the hearts of the fans. The instruments came together in a beautiful tragedy of angst and love.

Lila knew exactly what she wanted when she looked up at Layne on stage and this was it. Engulfed in the parallel universe of her own dreams, she felt them come alive and merge with her real life. A wave of bliss and serenity washed over her as she watched the band. Her arms felt nearly detached from her body as they swayed above her head to the rhythm of the music. She danced between Katelyn and Stacy, hoping for this moment to never end. They were all drunk and happy, and having the time of their lives.

Song after song, Layne belted out the lyrics, holding nothing back. He commanded the crowd the only way he knew how as he fed off their energy. This night was different, there was more excitement in the air than he had ever seen before, which only pushed him more and more. The band stopped mid song for the drum solo, only this time, Layne joined in with a guitar solo as well. The crowd cried out with cheers as the guitar battled the drums. Layne and Joe watched each other for queues of where each was going next. Thompson sensed a gap and filled in with his impromptu bass lines as the fans begged for more. Layne ran to the edge of the drum set, taunting Joe as the solos intensified. Thompson stood his ground with a wide stance, pounding away at his bass. Finally, when Layne felt the crowd could not possibly take anymore, he sprinted to his microphone just in time to finish the last chorus. The ending drew out the instruments as the crowd roared. Layne knew they had them right where he wanted them.

Lila watched as Lee raced onstage to hand Layne his black guitar that had been rebuilt earlier in the day. She wondered why he was bringing it out now instead of coming back for an encore. She watched on as the song started, realizing that she had lost track of how many songs they had played. Layne toyed with the crowd, pretending to remove his guitar throughout the song. The crowd waited in anticipation knowing that he would destroy the guitar on stage. Each time he lifted the guitar, more screams rang throughout the room. He lifted a hand to his ear as if he could not hear them and the crowd let out a deafening roar. The band played the last chorus three times, begging the crowd's reaction. With the excitement and anticipation at its absolute peak, Layne let loose a disturbingly beautiful scream as the guitar was raised above his head and crashed down onto the stage. Debris flew across the stage with the explosions as Layne beat the guitar to death. The crowd egged him on with every blow. The neck snapped from the body of the guitar and was held together only by the strings as the pieces flew around. He suddenly turned and launched the remainder of the guitar full force into the drum set. Joe was caught off guard as cymbals and stands went flying around him. Joe quickly joined in as he saw Thompson preparing his bass, holding the guitar by the neck as if it were a baseball bat. Joe pitched the snare drum straight towards him as Thompson hit a homerun across the stage, leaving a broken and disfigured snare limping about. The entire room erupted in applause as the three took a bow on stage. Layne ran to his microphone to say his goodbyes to the crowd.

"That was our last song of the night!" he screamed out, competing with the crowd. "But don't worry! That's definitely not the end of the show! We have a surprise for everyone here tonight! I'm sure by now you have all heard the rumors and I can tell you that we do have a special guest here tonight! So we are going to get the fuck off the stage so we can let them play! Thank you so much for coming out!" The band waved and cheered, pretending to blow kisses as they left the stage.

Katelyn grabbed Lila and Stacy, rushing them through the crowd. She quickly motioned for Jeff and Nicole to follow before losing sight of them. Katelyn had to force a path through since no one was about to leave before finding out who was going to perform. They finally made their way to the security guard separating them from the backstage door. Lila was amazed at the constant volume of the crowd. Once they were through the backstage door her ears had a moment to rest.

"That was absolutely amazing!" Lila shouted as she wrapped her arms around Layne.

He had a towel around his neck, trying his best to wipe the sweat off. "Yeah! That was incredible!" he yelled as he looked towards Thompson and Joe. "Dude! You guys did amazing out there!" he complimented as they rubbed their faces with towels.

"Yeah, I have a good feeling about that one," Thompson replied, with his face buried in a towel. "That just might have been our best one yet.

"It better have been!" Joe exclaimed while he dried his hair. "We basically destroyed all of our instruments tonight!"

The band let out a nervous laugh as they each quietly calculated how expensive their stunt may have been. Katelyn prepared the shots from the brand new bottle of whiskey as the band finished drying themselves off. Stacy could not help but admire the adorable sight of each band member holding their special someone. Lila was tight in Layne's arms as she stared deep into his eyes. Jeff gripped Thompson lovingly as he complimented Thompson on the show. Nicole smothered Joe in kisses while telling him how great of a drummer he was.

Katelyn shattered the moment once the alcohol was ready. She quickly passed the shot glasses around to each person before saying a toast. "Here's to you guys having another great show and as always, an amazing night to come!"

Everyone cheered as the shots were taken. The energy was still incredibly high as the band asked for another shot. Suddenly a voice rang out from across the room as someone walked towards the group.

"Hey! How in the hell are we supposed to follow a set like that?" the guitarist joked as his band walked into the room.

The group stood star struck and speechless as the band approached.

Katelyn slowly moved forward to introduce herself when suddenly the realization hit her all at once. "Oh my god! You're Lars Frederiksen!" she exclaimed as she fiercely shook his hand. "And your Tim Armstrong!" she added as she moved to the next. "This is Matt Freeman!" she exclaimed to everyone as she nearly missed the hand shake. "And you're Branden Steineckert!" Katelyn was in such shock that she did not know what more to say.

"Yeah you're right. We're the band Rancid," Lars proudly stated.

Layne quickly introduced Lila, Stacy, Nicole and Jeff, as they were lost in the excitement. They stood nearly frozen as they met their idols. When they were finally able to speak, they each took turns telling the band how much they enjoyed their music in great detail.

Lars laughed at their reactions, "We are always glad to meet our fans." He quickly turned to Layne. "But really though, that was an amazing show. We were all blown away."

"Thank you so much," Layne replied. "That really means a lot to us, especially coming from you guys."

Lars thought for a moment, "I'll have to get your number, we may be able to put you guys in contact with some people. How long did you say you guys have been playing? About a year now?"

"Yeah!" Layne replied with his famous grin on his face. "That would be awesome!"

"Well that's really an impression, you definitely know how to entertain a crowd," Lars complimented as he turned to the rest of his band. "Well, you guys ready to go play!"

"Thank you so much!" Layne said again. "We are going to hurry up and get in the audience so we don't miss anything!"

Layne quickly rounded up the group as they headed for the backstage door. Layne shook hands as the crowd parted, forming an easy walk way for the group to navigate directly back to the center stage. As soon as they reached Katherine, Kate, Timothy, James and Gregory, praise, hugs and handshakes were given to the entire band. They gathered in complimenting the band as the lights dimmed and the crowd roared with excitement.

Dark figures took the stage as the crowd screamed with excitement. The anticipation was on the edge of bursting as multiple guitars were strummed in the darkness. The crowd hit a new level of audibility. The drums and bass crept their way in as the lights sprang on, revealing a large banner behind the stage that read 'Rancid'. Fans nearly exploded when they finally realized who were on stage. Without any announcement, Rancid burst into their first song of the night. Sound and music poured over the crowd as they cheered. The pit was alive with its own living breathing energy as the fans danced around the room.

Layne and Lila were squished against the stage as they looked up at the band. Layne protected Lila with his body while the crowd pushed and shoved all around them. Lila was captivated in the moment. Not only did she enjoy the punk rock music, but also now she was with the boy she loved as he held her tight, protecting her from all the madness around them. She felt as if time slowed down whenever she was in his arms. She watched as the world went on around her, taking in every bit of the moment. She loved the way her body felt pressed against his. The worries of yesterday seemed like a distant memory that was replaced by happiness. Lila knew in this moment that she was in love with him. She loved his shy and awkwardness when they were alone, and the way he could light up a room just by walking in. She thought about how it did not matter if he was in a band or not, even though that was a huge bonus she thought to herself, she wanted nothing more than to be with him no matter what was happening.

Layne watched the band on stage intently; having no idea what Lila was thinking until she suddenly turned around and kissed him. He knew instinctively that this was not a normal kiss. In his mind, the cheering crowd was no longer focused on the music, but instead, cheering for him and Lila. In his imaginative world, the music around him changed from punk rock to a beautiful symphony. Violins and cellos crept out of the darkness on stage as sweet harmonics flowed around through the air. A conductor waved his hands elegantly as the music accented the curves of Lila's body. Cymbals crashed and banged simulating the imaginary fireworks flying over Layne's head as Lila's sweet and sensual lips caressed his.

As the first song ended, Tim Armstrong's voice brought Layne back in reality. "We are glad to be here tonight!" Tim Armstrong yelled as he competed with the screaming fans. "We are the band Rancid and we have a great show for you guys!" He tried to yell out before the volume of the crowd overtook him.

On a count of four, the next song exploded into a wall of sound as guitars battled amongst the bass and drums. The vocals held a beautiful harmony with back and forth rhythms as the distorted guitars paved the way. The bass guitar held its own as it rattled everything in sight with its low notes. The drums were fierce as they pounded away the backbeat of the rhythm with the cymbals crashing over the top. The years of experience showed as the band kept their instruments tight in the timing of each line, controlling the chaos with ease. The crowd sang along as loud as humanly possibly, knowing every word to every song. The voices combined to form a choir, which seemed to be made of thousands, as each song was played. The pit never let up, not even between songs. At any given moment, the fans were still in full party-mode with or without the music.

One by one, the men slowly joined the pit until the only ones left in the group were the girls. Lila and Stacy watched the band playing, and then would turn to the pit to laugh and point at the boys as they ran through the crowd, pushing and brawling as they went. The girls entertained themselves, dancing and rubbing on one another as they protected their perfect place in front of the stage until the boys made it safely back to the group. The girls comforted them as the boys showed off their newly acquired battle scars. Lila kissed Layne's arm just above a throbbing red scratch as he tried to play it off like it did not hurt. A simple kiss on the lips was all he needed to forget any pain he may have felt.

An hour easily slipped by without Layne being able to grasp the concept of time. He had nearly forgotten that he was going to sing with the band until a booming voice came through the microphone as a song ended.

"Man!" Tim Armstrong screamed out into the crowd. "You guys have to be the wildest audience we have ever seen!" The crowd erupted with cheer.

"That's for sure!" Lars Frederiksen joked into his microphone.

"Well we want to do something else special for you guys!" Tim Armstrong announced. "We want to bring our new friends up here to sing the next song with us. Layne! Thompson! Joe! Where you guys at?" he screamed into the microphone.

The crowd erupted as Layne, Thompson and Joe climbed from the audience onto the stage. They were rushed microphones while they chatted with the band. Once ready, the opening chords to the song rang out across the room.

"This is a song called Ruby Soho. Sing along if you know the word," Tim Armstrong cried out over the roar of the fans as he prepared to sing the first line. "Echoes of reggae," he sang as the audience joined in.

"Coming through my bedroom wall," Layne finishes the line as the room comes alive with cheers.

As they reached the chorus, both bands joined in the singing as well as all the screaming fans. Layne walked to the edge of the stage and sang directly to Lila, causing her heart to skip a beat before running back to the center of the stage. By this time, Joe and Thompson were waving their arms, encouraging the crowd to sing as loud as possible. The deafening screams from the fans shook the entire building as everyone danced about to the music.

After the song, Tim Armstrong thanked Layne, Thompson, and Joe as they climbed back down into the crowd. He thanked the audience as the band made their way off of the stage. With the energy level still at its peak, the fans made it clear they were not ready for the music to be over.

A chant started through the crowd as it spread like wildfire. The crowd was not ready to stop and they screamed for more. Finally, after a few minutes off stage, Rancid ran back on as the crowd was pleased. The audience had grown so loud, that the next few songs were nearly inaudible, while no one seemed to care. The pit quickly took form as the music rang out. The audience used the very last of their energy as the songs played. Layne could not help, but look around and admire the beauty he saw in it all. He was amazed how music could transform different people from all walks of life, bringing them together to share in the experience of the moment.

"Thank you so much!" Tim Armstrong called out as the last of the guitar feedback rang throughout the crowd. "We had a great time! I hope you all enjoyed it! We'll definitely make a trip back here to do it again!" he added as the band waved their final goodbyes and left the stage.

The energy was still high in the room as everyone came to the realization of the experience they had just witnessed. The group hung around the front of the stage for a few minutes as they reminisced in the memories of the night. As the crowd began to thin, the group made their way to the backstage door. Layne was the first through the door as he realized that Rancid was waiting for them. The group quickly rushed to the band and congratulated them. Praise was given all around as everyone talked about the show.

Lars Frederiksen turned to Layne as everyone mingled, "That was a great show, I'll seriously talk to some people and see what we can do for you guys. I talked to Tiffany during your set and got her contact info."

"That would be incredible!" Layne exclaimed, unable to hold back his enthusiasm.

"We have a tour coming up, so we will be busy for awhile, but I'll definitely see what we can do," Lars said as he shook his hand. "We have to get going, we've got a nice and slow bus ride back over the hill to the bay."

And just like that, Rancid was gone, leaving the group with their memories as they disappeared out of the building.

The group stuck around to help load the equipment in order to speed up the process. The plans for the night were made as the amplifiers and what was left of the drum set were loaded into the back of the truck. Lila and Stacy climbed into the mustang with Layne as the rest of the group piled into cars and they were off into the night.

CHAPTER 12

Stacy twisted and squirmed in her drunken state across the backseat, reliving the night's nostalgia. Lila tried her best to keep Stacy situated in a decent position with her body turned towards the back of the car while Layne drove through the night.

"That was amazing!" Stacy cried out as she fell across the seats while Lila's hand was just out of range.

Intoxicated by the event and the alcohol Stacy cried out followed by a hiccup, "Layne! I'm so glad we met you. Who would have thought?" Stacy tried her best to continue her sentence as her head dropped and she regained sobriety for the moment. "Who would have thought that when we met you on a train you would turn out to be this amazing person."

He laughed at the acknowledgement as the car sped through the night. Lila had one hand dedicated to Stacy, worried she would collapse in the backseat, while the other hand shifted focus to the radio. She took turns from being a concerned mother to a rock and roll goddess as she sang in perfect key along to every song.

Layne watched her with a desiring eye. "You haven't told me how well you can sing," he belted out as the car shifted from second to third gear.

"What?" Lila boosted with confidence. "I can't tell you all of my secrets on the first date," she joked as she gave Layne a wink.

As the mustang approached Thompson's house Lila let out a sigh of relief. She opened the car door only to find Stacy stumbling about.

"I'm fine. I can do it myself," Stacy Stated with great pride as she exited the car.

Joe's truck arrived with the equipment as Layne realized the party was in full swing inside the house.

"What's going on?" Layne asked, confused. "The party is here tonight?"

Lila laughed, "Yeah, James and Timothy set a bunch of stuff up while you were at the sound check earlier today."

"Really?" Layne added. "I had no idea we would be here tonight. I assumed we would have a party at James' like always."

Lila smirked while shooting Layne another wink. "You're not the only one with surprises," she joked as she grabbed his hand.

Stacy led the couple to Joe's truck while instructing them to unload the vehicle to get the party started. Layne and Lila laughed at her remarks while they did exactly what they were told. An assembly line of bodies made quick work of the unloading process. Soon the group filled the basement with the amplifiers, guitars and drums. Just above their heads, the party raged on. Music, bass, noise of laughter and singing seeped through the floorboards as the group took a moment to stare at the ceiling of the basement.

As everyone turned to join the party, Thompson expressed his concern for the noise, "Oh lord, the damn police will be stopping by at any moment because of this."

Joe laughed at the comment, "Then we better hurry up and get up there before the party is over!"

Stacy led the way into the house with a confident drunk stumble. Lila followed behind her, still worried that she may fall over at any moment. Layne was the first of the band through the door followed by Joe and Thompson. Nicole and Jeff brought up the rear of the group.

Kate and Katelyn were already in the kitchen with drinks poured and ready, awaiting the groups' arrival. Kate quickly passed around the cups while Katelyn instructed that the epicenter of the party was in the front living room. Layne, Thompson and Joe were confused of how music would be coming so loud from that room, while the music was usually played through the amplifiers in the basement. Stacy announced that she was leading the way through the house and with a glass raised above her head, left the kitchen.

Lila grabbed Layne's hand, "Come on, let's go see what all the fuss is about."

He followed her heartwarming smiling through the door into the dining room. As soon as he entered, the room came alive. The guests in the room flocked to him shouting praise and congratulations on another amazing night. As soon as Thompson and Joe entered, they were surrounded as well with excited friends and guests. Stacy was in a momentary shock as she snapped out of her drunken state. She watched intently as Layne, Joe and Thompson stood before her, almost appearing to glow within the room. She focused on the way they each interacted with their audience almost as if they were back on stage in front of a full crowd.

"Is it always like this?" Stacy whispered to Lila who had stepped off to the side, narrowly escaping the stampede.

"Yeah," Lila laughed as she watched Layne without ever breaking her focus from him. "Isn't it amazing?"

Layne slowly made his way to Lila to give her a kiss. She felt the electricity and energy that kept him alive, pulsing through his veins as his lips touched hers. She had never felt so comfortable in another person's arms. A shot of alcohol was handed to Layne as he quickly took it without hesitation before giving Lila another kiss. She could taste the sweet sugary rum as she kissed him back.

"Hey!" Joe shouted through the room. "Let's go see what all this music is about!" he added as him and Thompson tried to push their way through the crowd. Shouts of excitement rang through the room as Thompson and Joe rejoined Layne.

Stacy took her queue and led the group to the next room, only to have the scene play out as it had before. Now even more people were gathered around the band and the music played louder as they drew closer to the source. Stacy was finally able to regain control after the band was hounded with excitement. She led into the hallway, now ever so close to the source of the music. Layne noted that something about it was not just a recording. The songs were switching about at an impressive speed while playing on the hooks to the songs. Layne was confused as to how it was possible.

Lila glowed in the black lights strung across the hallway as her t-shirt beneath her flannel sprang to life. Layne could hardly see past Stacy with her bouncing walk down the hall. He caught glimpses of a room so packed that people were standing at the end of the hallway just to be near the action. Stacy weaseled her way into the room and disappeared into the crowd. Layne finally got the chance to peek into the living room looking out over Lila's head before she pushed her way into the crowd. He quickly noticed that the table and chairs that occupied most of the room earlier in the day had been removed and a full dance party equipped with black lights and lasers filled their place. Across the room in front of the fireplace stood a DJ at a table between two towers of speakers. He was fast at work mixing records. Layne quickly pushed his way through the room, undetected by the guests as he made his way to the DJ.

"Jeremy!" Layne cried out over the music as he shook his hand. "Dude this is awesome! I didn't know you were bringing your equipment over tonight!"

"Yeah, I wanted to do something a little special for you guys tonight," Jeremy replied without missing a beat. "I talked to Tim and James last night and they thought it would be a good idea to have the party here tonight."

"This is great man, I had no idea. This is really cool," Layne replied, ecstatic with the surprise.

"I got over to James' kind of late last night and ended up missing you. They said you went to bed early, what was that all about?" Jeremy teased.

"Oh man, I didn't know I missed you, sorry about that," Layne screamed over the music. "I was putting Lila to bed and ended up falling asleep," he assured.

Jeremy laughed at his excuse, "Yeah, I'm sure that's exactly how it happened."

Layne finished his cup of alcohol and looked down into the empty cup almost saddened that it was gone. Jeremy noticed his despair and offered his help. "Someone get this man a beer!" Jeremy shouted into the room while pointing at Layne.

Soon the realization that Layne stood before them hit the crowd as cheers rang out. Beer came flying through the crowd almost instantly as Layne was amazed by the efficiency of Jeremy's plan. Joe and Thompson stepped into the room just in time to take the main focus off of Layne. Joe shouted that he needed a beer as well and two cans made their way through the crowd to Thompson and Joe. Everyone cheered as Jeremy cut the music to congratulate the band on an amazing show, also adding in how amazing and surprising Rancid was to be there as well. Screams filled the house with excitement as the music came flowing through the speakers.

Lila pushed her way through the crowd and grabbed Layne's arm. She wanted to dance and she was not going to take no for an answer. He was reluctantly dragged to the center of the room without putting up a protest. As she turned to him, his anxiety subsided. His fear was replaced by a calming peaceful warmth throughout his soul as he lost himself in her eyes. Lila moved gracefully to the music before him, causing the rhythm to flow through his body. A smile formed across his face as she led the way. Suddenly, nothing around him mattered as the world fell away, leaving just the two of them alone. Together they danced and moved as one to the melody of their heartbeats. The rhythm of the bass formed on his longing desires for her. He studied her body inventively with every sway of her hips. His hands found themselves caressing the curves of her waist with a light touching, careful not to interrupt her movements. She stared deep into his soft eyes as she felt the love flowing through her body.

Lila focused on his lips patiently waiting for the next kiss, longing for the feel upon her skin. She spun in his arms, pressing her back against his chest, hoping to be as close as possible to him. He gently kissed her neck as it sent sensual shivers down her spine, fueling the euphoria. She could feel them alone in a world of their own creation and she never wanted to leave. Spinning back around to face him, her hands explored his body as her hips set the pace. Every touch left him tingling for more as he pulled her closer. With her body pressed tightly against his, she wrapped her arms around his neck and without a word, promised to never let go. He studied her lips as the two swayed as one on the dance floor. The tension built to its exploding point before he finally kissed her.

Lila whispered softly into his ear. "I need you now," she said, as her heart longed for his.

Ideas raced through his mind as he thought of where they could be alone. "We can go upstairs," he stated quickly as she gently kissed his neck.

Replying with just a smile, Lila grabbed his hand and whisked him away. She hit the hallway without slowing down, quickly finding a path through the people who stood in her way. With a firm grip on Layne's hand, she headed across the next room towards the stairs.

Jeff was excited to see Lila and Layne as he offered a drink while displaying a bottle of whiskey in his hand. "Lila would you like a drink?" he asked caringly.

Lila grabbed the bottle out of Jeff's hand and thanked him as she pulled Layne up the stairs, leaving Jeff with a confused and puzzled look across his face.

"What just happened?" Nicole laughed as she looked at Jeff.

"I have no idea!" he replied as he stared helplessly towards the empty stairs. "Looks like they must be having a party for two," he winked as he turned towards Nicole.

She laughed, "I'm sure we can find another bottle in the kitchen."

Layne slammed the bedroom door shut behind him as Lila attacked him. Kisses flew around touching lips, cheeks, and necks as they stumbled through the room. Layne eyed their destination as a futon in the corner of the room in the shape of a couch. Lila tripped and nearly fell over an armchair. She was not detoured. Lila's flannel jacket flew across the room as Layne carefully removed his. The bottle cap to the whiskey sprang across the floor as Lila pulled a shot from the bottle and handed it over to Layne. With a fierce look of burning passion, she ripped off her shirt as he took a shot. She then quickly helped to remove Layne's shirt as her fingertips raced across his chest. The two gained momentum as they reached the futon. Layne unbuckled his belt and ripped it through the loops as Lila fought to get her legs out of her tight jeans. He stood over Lila as she sat in her sexy black lingerie on the couch.

"DUDE!" Timothy's voice boomed through the room, freezing Layne and Lila in their tracks. "Give us a second to get out of here first!"

Layne finally noticed the door to the smoking room cracked open with Timothy in the doorway. He gave a frantic look towards Layne and Lila as laughter rang out behind him. Lila nearly died from embarrassment as she tried to use her shirt to cover herself up.

Timothy tried to hide his laughter to help Lila. "I'm so sorry," he said with a hand covering his mouth and turning his attention back into the room. "Everyone grab your drinks, we're headed downstairs."

Layne found his flannel and covered Lila's legs as she sat partially covered on the couch. He then took a sip of whiskey and offered the bottle to Lila, which she quickly grabbed out of his hand. Seeing the hilarious side of the situation, Layne could not help but stand with his pants undone and shirt off in the middle of the room as Timothy, James, Kate, and Katherine shamefully exited the small smoking room adjacent to the bedroom. He quickly tried his best to turn their attention towards him as he began stretching his legs in the center of the room.

"What the hell are you doing?" James asked confused.

"Stretching," Layne said without stopping. "Don't you know that you have to stretch before a strenuous activity?" he asked playfully.

His distraction began to work as even Lila, who had buried her head in her hands, began to laugh along at Layne's ridiculous stretches.

Timothy and James were quickly out of the bedroom door as Kate and Katherine apologized to Lila as they left the room, trying not to make the scene any worse.

The door to the smoking room was now wide open with puckering sounds still coming from the room. Layne and Lila slowly craned their necks to look inside only to see Lee and Stacy making out in the corner.

"Sorry bro," Lee said as soon as he realized they were being watched and without a word led Stacy out the window onto the second story balcony.

For a moment Lila was confused and was going to question what she just saw. Instead she quickly shook her head to forget the thoughts of the bizarre situation and focused her attention back onto Layne who had just as puzzled a look upon his face.

As soon as Lila and Layne were alone again, she questioned his interesting reaction, "Stretching? That's the first thing that popped into your head?" She giggled as she took a sip from the bottle as her embarrassment lifted and she started to realize the humor in it all.

"It's the only thing I could think of in the moment," he replied as she handed him the bottle.

Lila smiled playfully, "You are too much sometimes."

Layne reached down and slowly pulled the articles of clothing from Lila's body. "I believe we were in the middle of something before we were rudely interrupted," he whispered, gently kissing her lips.

"I believe we were," she replied.

It was late in the night when Layne and Lila emerged from the room. The music had been done for some time now and the party had all but been broken up. A few stragglers lined the rooms as Layne and Lila made their way through the house. Familiar voices echoed the hall as they approached the Turkish room.

"About time you two join the party," Katelyn announced as Lila and Layne walked in.

Katelyn kneeled in the center of the room next to the coffee table with her beautifully cut lines of cocaine across a silver platter. Nicole, Joe, Jeff and Thompson were squished together on the couch laughing and joking about how long Layne and Lila had been missing. James and Timothy shared an end table that was barely big enough for a makeshift seat in the corner of the room. Stacy and Kate were seated in chairs next to the window chatting amongst themselves at lightning speed. Layne found an open chair that was left by Katelyn and gestured for Lila to sit on his lap to save room.

"Yeah, yeah, yeah," Layne replied to Katelyn with a smirk across his face. "Where's Greg and Katherine? Are they off hiding somewhere?"

Katelyn giggled as she replied, "They left together a little while ago."

"Hmm. I wonder what they're up too," Nicole remarked as everyone jumped to conclusions.

"Layne, you need a beer?" Joe asked as he produced a beer from a case in front of the couch.

"Yeah that would be great," Layne replied, reaching out his hand. "You have a smoke?"

"Yeah. I've got you buddy," Joe said as he pulled a cigarette from his pack.

Lila had been listening to Kate and Stacy's conversation as she tried desperately to keep up with their pace. "Stacy, how are you still awake?" She finally asked. "The last time I saw you, you were drinking water because you were about ready to fall over."

Stacy's eyes filled with excitement. "Oh don't worry about me, I feel great! Greater than great. Like really, really great," she assured as she continued on with her rant.

Katelyn butted in, "Don't worry I've been taking care of her."

Lila was nearly mortified. "Did you give her some coke?"

"Just a little," Katelyn replied. "But not very much, I promise, especially for her first time."

Layne sensed Lila's tension, "It's okay sweetheart, Katelyn is a pro at this, I'm sure she didn't let her do too much."

Thompson joined in, "Yeah I saw it, Stacy did about half a line over an hour ago. There's actually no way that she still feels it, she must be running on adrenaline at this point."

Lila calmed down as everyone in the room began laughing along.

"By the way," Katelyn added, "Stacy is awesome! She's definitely one of us."

"Yeah!" James blurted out. "Just like you Lila."

Lila felt warm and relaxed as she thanked them for the kind gesture. "I'm really glad I got to meet all of you, this has been an amazing weekend."

The group joked and talked about the events of the weekend late into the night before slowly peeling off to find places throughout the house to sleep. Kate and Katelyn left to find a bed to share leaving James and Timothy behind. Joe and Nicole took their usual bedroom upstairs when Thompson and Jeff decided to call it a night. Lila invited Stacy to share the futon bed with her and Layne as they made their way back up the stairs.

CHAPTER 13

Layne awoke from the morning light shining through the window. He looked across Lila's body as she illuminated beneath his arms. He kissed her cheek as he felt the gentle warmth of the morning sun. Rolling over slowly, careful not to wake Lila with his movement, he found Stacy beside him as she lay, wrapped tightly in a blanket next to the wall. He silently chuckled to himself as he remembered how she had gotten there. He laid there between the two girls for a few minutes as the hangover built within his body and reminisced on the night before. Lila awoke as she rolled over into Layne's arms, feeling safe once again.

"Good morning Lila," he whispered in a calm loving voice.

"Good morning," she smiled back.

Lila stretched her arms and legs out as the sun touched her skin, re-energizing her body. Layne watched as this goddess beside him gracefully moved in his arms. She grabbed his hand and kissed it before snuggling in close to him.

"What time is it?" she asked as she closed her eyes tight.

"I'm not sure, I haven't gotten up to check yet," Layne replied as he played with her hair. "But we should probably get some food."

Lila felt her stomach aching. "I'm not sure if I can even eat right now. My body feels like I got ran over by a truck," she said as she held her stomach.

Layne chuckled to himself, "I'm so sorry, but I was very impressed how you held your alcohol this weekend."

"With all the excitement, it would be hard not to keep going," she remarked.

They lay there in bed talking about the concert from the night before, each focusing and telling the other about the different parts of the event. Layne had the chance to explain how hard it was for him not to ruin the secret of the guest performance as soon as he found out. Lila's eyes filled with excitement when she relived what it was like to meet Rancid backstage and they both remembered how shocked Katelyn had been.

"Can I ask you a question?" Lila asked with her adorable eyes as she looked up at Layne.

He felt slightly uncomfortable as to what this question may lead. "Sure, anything, what's on your mind?" he said as he tried to play cool while waiting for what she may ask.

"What's the story between you and Katelyn?" Lila asked, not sure how to word the question the way she wanted.

"She's one of my best friends. Why? What do you mean?" he replied, not sure on what to say.

"I mean, I've seen you with the other girls that you're friends with and you and Katelyn act differently." She paused for a moment to gather her thoughts. "Like at the show, you're friends say that you never bring girls along to the show, but Katelyn is special and she always gets a backstage pass." She paused for another moment as she thought about what she could add. "I'm not trying to be the jealous 'girlfriend' or anything, I just want to know more about you. After all, it's really only been two days since I met you Layne Michael," Lila finished with a smile.

He laughed when he realized that the weekend felt like a lifetime they had been together. "Well, you know that we were all friends from high school," Layne began. "And after my last serious relationship, everyone was there, but it felt like no one was there," he tried to think of how to better explain himself. "Like we all still hung out, but no one knew what to do or say when I would get stuck in these different moods, I guess you could say."

After a short pause Layne found a way to relate his words to her, "It was like I was stuck on this crazy wild rollercoaster, and instead of anyone trying to help get me off, they just jumped on and went for the ride with me, because they didn't know what else to do. I didn't know what else to do." Layne kissed Lila's hand as he dug through his memories of the past. "Katelyn was the one that helped me through it, kind of in her own way, coached me through it. So that's why I've always been grateful to her and I cherish her friendship. She looked over me when I was down and protected me when I was weak. I know that I can count on her for anything."

Lila did not know what to say. She had wanted to know more, but she was not quite ready for this. "Why didn't you ever date her?" she said without thinking. "I mean, not trying to be rude, but you two seem to have a special relationship."

Layne laughed at her comment, "Yeah, we do have a special relationship, but we are just friends. A long time ago I did think about that and I just couldn't."

"Why not?" Lila intrigued.

"Well, I was hurt and upset and Katelyn was there for me, but I felt that if we dated then I would just be using her to make myself feel better and that wasn't right. She's way too good of a person for that. My heart had belonged to someone else at the time and I just didn't have those feelings towards Katelyn." He looked down to gauge his response from Lila's face.

"I understand," she smirked. "You were just some wild crazy boy all the girls wanted to be with."

"Oh shut up!" he said playfully as Lila tried to pin him down for a kiss and he pretended to hold her back.

"I am sorry you had to go through all of that," Lila stated sincerely. "I couldn't imagine someone hurting another person like that," she added.

"It's okay. I made it through all of that, and I wouldn't change it for the world because even after everything, I have a wonderful life and a beautifully wonderful girl right here by my side," he replied as he kissed her passionately. "Shall we go get some food?"

"We shall," she replied with a warm smile.

"I'll see if Stacy wants something to eat," Layne added as he rolled over towards Stacy. He slowly inched his face closer until he was nose to nose with her face and whispered, "Stacy." After a moment she did not budge so he tried again a little louder, "Staaaaccccyyy."

Lila laughed at Layne's failed efforts to wake her, "Be nice to Stacy, she had a long day."

Layne ignored her while he tried again. "Stacy!" he said in a stern voice.

Stacy shook and opened her eyes, trying her best to focus on what was in front of her to no avail. She quickly wiggled and squirmed her head away, but found that her body was trapped inside the blanket. Lila and Layne started laughing as soon as Stacy realized she was stuck.

"That is not funny!" Stacy demanded. "You nearly gave me a heart attack," she added as she unwound the blanket. Lila and Layne could not help, but laugh hysterically. "Why did you guys wake me up anyway?" Stacy demanded.

Layne wiped his eyes with his hands, mustering the energy to reply, "We are going to get some food. Would you like to go with us or do you want us to bring you some back?"

"Just get me something. Whatever you guys get." Stacy said, grumpily as she rolled over and went back to sleep.

Layne climbed off the bed and found his pants where he had laid them neatly the night before. Reaching in his pocket for his phone, he checked the time to the realization that it was 11:00 am. Lila followed Layne down the stairs and through the eerily quiet house. Rooms were filled with cups, beer cans and bottles as they navigated through the remains of the party. Sleeping bodies filled chairs and couches as they walked room-to-room, taking inventory of the remaining guests. Soon they were out the door.

Layne pulled his sunglasses over his precious eyes as he exited the house. Lila followed suit, careful to not let the sun's rays attack her delicate face. The air was calm and warm as they stepped out onto the porch. Lila watched as Layne's flannel flowed effortlessly across his body as he glided towards the street. As he reached the car, he carefully opened the passenger door and waited for Lila with a patient smile.

"Thank you," Lila announced as she climbed down into the mustang. "What a gentleman," she praised.

Layne swiftly made his way to the driver's seat and they sped off into the cool morning. Static filled the car as the radio turned on, followed by the elegantly sharp guitar intro to the song "Santa Monica" by Everclear. Lila jumped in elation as she informed Layne how much she loved the song. This filled his heart with joy as he sang along to the song just for her.

"We could live beside the ocean, leave the fire behind, swim out past the breakers and watch the world die," Layne echoed through the car as Lila sang and danced along.

He felt as if he were watching in slow motion as she used her entire body to emphasize each word of the song. As she turned towards him, her glasses caught the reflection of the road as the path ahead stared back at him through her eyes. The sun's beams pierced through the windshield, igniting Lila's alluring dark hair in a fiery glow.

She watched Layne as he effortlessly shifted the stick shift through the gears without ever missing a beat of the song. She noted how he was holding nothing back now. Even with his driver window rolled down and wind whipping passed the car, Lila felt his deep booming voice transcend her body as she was overcome with bliss.

"Where's your camera at?" Layne asked as the song ended.

"I put it with my bags in the trunk last night before the show," Lila stated. "I used up the first roll already, I wanted to see how well it works," Lila added.

"Good. I was wondering if you had a chance too," Layne replied as he hatched an idea. "We can make a quick stop on the way and get the film developed if you would like."

Lila's eyes filled with excitement and surprise. "Yes!" Lila exclaimed as she grabbed his arm. "Let's do it! Is there a place around here?"

Layne chuckled, as he had not expected her response to be so animated. "Yeah, there's still an old photo shop here just down the street."

Lila gripped his arm tightly as she imagined how the photos would turn out. Still filled with joy as the car pulled off the road and into a parking space, she quickly ran to the trunk to retrieve her camera. Layne calmly walked to the back of the mustang to casually open the trunk while Lila was nearly bursting out of her skin. With the camera safely in her hands, she led the way into the shop, nearly leaving Layne behind.

Layne walked into the shop to find the walls covered with photographs ranging from all sizes and styles. The soft lighting in the room truly brought the photographs to life as he tried his best to study each image. Some were famous photos he had seen before such as pictures from Yosemite taken by Ansel Adams. Others must have been local photographers, he thought to himself. He recognized the roads, bridges and parks that had been captured in the photographs as all being from around Stockton. He watched as Lila made her way hastily through the room to a man standing behind a counter.

"Good morning," the old man greeted Lila as she neared. "What can I do for you today?"

"Good morning," Lila said with a warm smile as she set the camera on the counter before him. "Do you develop film here?" she inquired as she read the name Dennis across his nametag.

Dennis smiled as he saw the camera set before him. "Yes we do. You came to the right place," he replied. "Where did you get this? This is a very nice camera, it's an Exakta Varex."

Lila ignited with excitement. "We got it at a thrift store on Saturday. I took some pictures and wanted to see if it was working correctly."

Astounded by the answer, Dennis replied, "You had a very lucky find with this one." He picked up the camera to carefully inspect it. "And it seems to be in great condition, hardly any of the normal wear and tear."

Lila was pleased by this. "My grandfather had one just like it, so when I saw it I just had to have it."

"Well he must have had good taste as well then," Dennis commented with a smile. "We can get your film started right now," he added as he turned towards the back of the shop. "Martha," he called out. "Martha, I have some film for you." The old man gently opened the camera and removed the film roll as Martha appeared from the back of the shop.

"Good morning sweetie," Martha said to Lila as she walked towards her husband to retrieve the film.

By this time Layne had slowly made his way around the room, marveling at the photographs, as he approached the group at the counter.

Martha had a soft look in her eye, the way a grandmother awes over her grandchildren. "And who is this?" she asked as she saw Layne.

Layne calmly smiled as Lila responded. "This," she started, as she looked him over. "This is my boyfriend, Layne," she stated bashfully while staring at Layne.

"Oh," Martha said delightedly.

"Yes," Lila responded, as her heart skipped a beat just by looking at Layne. "He definitely is something special."

Martha could not help but admire the young couple. "I can start your film now and it should be done just under an hour."

"That would be great," Lila replied as she shifted her gaze back to Martha.

Martha said her goodbyes and took the film with her as she disappeared into the backroom.

"Is there anything else we could help you with today?" Dennis asked after Martha had left.

Lila looked around noticing all of the photographs that surrounded her. Mesmerized by the images, she slowly walked along the walls, recording each and every detail. The images captivated her as each and every one held its own story. She gazed at them as if they were individual little time capsules of the world as they captured subtle moments frozen in time. One caught her eye as she came to a complete stop before it. The photograph painted a picture of what seemed to be trees lining a small dirt road in the middle of fall. Lila admired the contrast of colors ranging from the golden yellows, faded greens, and darkened browns of the leaves falling from the trees, to the sparkling blues of the sky that peaked through the bare branches. She gazed and imagined what it would be like, standing there in that moment just before the picture was taken. Maybe the road led to a house, she thought, maybe a big magnificent house in the country. One with a small loving family surrounded by miles of open space to do as they pleased. That's where I want to live someday, she thought to herself.

"What are all these photos for?" Lila asked aloud, breaking her own daydream.

Dennis had been watching Lila browse the photographs on the wall. "This store is also a gallery for local photographers to showcase and sell their work," he replied. "Are there any that catch your attention?"

"Yes, this one with the autumn trees, it is absolutely beautiful," she answered without breaking her gaze.

Layne walked over to Lila, wanting to see which photograph she was eyeing. Without having to ask her, he instantly knew which one. The image had a calming effect over his soul as he stared into the photograph, getting lost amongst the scenery, almost as if he had seen it once before.

Lila turned to Layne, "I would love to live in a house with a driveway like this someday," she remarked. "Wouldn't it be amazing to see these beautiful trees every time you came home?" she imagined. "And drive along a dirt driveway all the way to the house."

"That would be perfect, wouldn't it?" he said soothingly.

Lila and Layne walked along the walls, deciphering the meanings behind the photos. Lila seemed to enjoy the scenery photographs the best and even pointed out her favorites with people mixed into the scene. Layne carefully listened and studied the way Lila described each image with her own interpretation. He admired the subtle details she was able to pick up on, ones he would have never noticed. He realized quickly how she was to photography as he was to music. He fell in love with her ideas and imagination as she created worlds from each of the works. He watched her intently as if she were a great painter, looking over other works of art.

When Lila was finished, they decided to pick up food while they waited for the film to be developed. Full of energy, Lila raced Layne to the car, completely without his knowledge, just to tease him on how slow he was. He laughed at her childish attitude as they climbed into the mustang. Lila scanned the radio, weeding out the midday commercials as Layne drove along. A few blocks away, he whipped the car into a Jack In The Box drive thru and pulled the car close to the speaker to call out the order.

"Welcome to Jack In The Box. How may I help you?" a grainy voice squeaked through the speaker.

"Yeah, can I have twenty tacos?" Layne requested, without consulting Lila.

Shocked, Lila quickly replied, "twenty? What on earth are you getting twenty tacos for?"

Before Layne could explain the grainy voice boomed back, "Okay, twenty tacos. Would you like anything else?"

"Yeah," Layne added onto the order. "A lot of taco sauce. Like a lot, a lot. We're going to need a grip of taco sauce," he added jokingly.

The grainy voice played along with the joke, "Okay, that'll be twenty tacos and a grip of hot sauce."

As the mustang pulled forward towards the window, Lila asked again, "What do we need twenty tacos for? And what's a grip of hot sauce?" She sat very confused and puzzled by the event that just took place.

Layne laughed at her confusion. "I'm getting tacos for everyone in the house," he announced proudly. "That's why we walked around this morning checking the rooms, I was counting how many people were left in the house. And a grip is a whole lot of hot sauce," he finished his statement by sticking his tongue out towards Lila.

Lila giggled, "You're ridiculous sometimes."

Lila rubbed his arm with her fingers as he paid for the food and was asked to pull around to the parking lot to wait for the tacos. The mustang was warm in the midday sun as it became apparent that sitting in the car for any extended amount of time would not be desirable.

Inside the restaurant, Lila found a table while Layne ordered sodas for the both of them. She picked a table overlooking the parking lot, as she watched over the shiny blue metallic mustang parked outside. As Layne brought the drinks to Lila, she noticed a group of teenagers, who had come into the fast food restaurant behind them, had started to whisper and stare in their direction.

"I think you have some admirers," Lila giggled as she sipped her drink.

Layne casually stole a quick glance at the group Lila was talking about. "Yeah, it seems to happen from time to time." He acted as if he was used to the attention, but really this was all new to him.

After a few minutes, the bravest of the group finally built up the courage to walk over towards Layne. "Are you Layne Michael?" he asked nervously.

"Yes I am," Layne greeted with a handshake and a warm smile.

"You're the lead singer of Bad Habits!" the teenager exclaimed.

Layne chuckled to himself, "Yeah, the last time I checked I was."

The teenager turned to his friends to relay the news as each of the group walked over to talk to Layne.

"We saw your show last night. It was amazing!" the teenager expressed as his friends had the chance to shake Layne's hand.

"Thank you very much," Layne replied. "I'm glad you enjoyed it." Layne pulled out a hand full of stickers for the teenagers, "Here you guys go."

"Thank you so much!" They exclaimed as they looked over the stickers as if it were some new found treasure. As soon as the food was ready, the group said their goodbyes, grabbed their food and left the restaurant in high spirits, leaving Layne all to Lila.

"Does that happen all the time?" Lila intrigued as she played with her straw in the cup.

"Not very often, but it does seem to be happening more and more," Layne answered as he relaxed down into his seat. "How do you feel about your boyfriend being famous?" Layne joked as he fidgeted his fingers in small drum patterns on the table.

"Who says I'm your girlfriend?" Lila smirked from behind her cup.

"You did!" Layne laughed. "You said it at the photography place," he added with his loving eyes.

"Well, I just didn't know what to say in the moment. I couldn't be like, this is some guy I met a few days ago that I kind of like and for some reason, trusted him enough to stay all weekend with him," Lila remarked as she tried to sarcastically simplify the events.

"What? You only kind of like me?" Layne laughed as he repeated the only part he heard her say.

Lila's cheeks slowly moved to a slight shade of red. "Maybe I like you a little more than that," she said while trying to hide her embarrassment.

"Do you like me enough to be my girlfriend?" Layne asked.

"Are you seriously asking me? Or just hypothetically?" she responded, cautious to give a real answer.

"Seriously," he replied. "As we sit in this lovely and beautiful five star Jack In The Box, the only thing I want more than some tacos is for you to be my girlfriend."

Even with his attempts at being funny and silly, Lila's heart filled with joy as he asked her. "I would kill for some tacos right now, and I would love to be your girlfriend," she answered with a sincere smile.

Layne's heart skipped a beat as he tried to hide his excitement. He could not help, but trace every curve of her face with his eyes so that he could remember this moment perfectly forever. He noted the way the sun's reflection from the glass window lit her face, accenting her natural beauty. How she elegantly presented herself even when no one was looking. He loved the warmth he felt inside his stomach from Lila just being there with him. It was one of the best feelings he had ever experienced, and he wanted more. Without a word, and faces full of bashful smiles, they leaned in to seal their relationship with a kiss.

As soon as the tacos were ready, Layne jumped up to retrieve them. Lila casually followed Layne out to the car as he danced around in excitement for his tacos. The mustang raced through the streets to the photography shop to retrieve the prints. It was Lila's turn to express her excitement as she jumped from the car and ran to the door, leaving Layne completely behind. He chuckled as he walked in, noticing that Lila was like a kid in a candy store as her pace picked up to a skip across the sidewalk and into the shop.

"Perfect timing," Dennis called out as Lila reached the far counter. "Martha just finished your photos."

Lila was ecstatic as she took the envelope from Dennis' hands. "Did they turn out okay?" she asked.

"I'm sure you'll be quite pleased with the results," Dennis replied with a warm smile.

Lila informed Layne that she did not want to open the photos until they got back to the house. As the mustang pulled away from it's parking spot, she begged him to drive as quickly as possible as she grew more and more anxious. He asked her why she would not just open them there and she stated that it would be more special if they opened them together.

As soon as the car stopped in front of Thompson's house, Lila clutched her envelope tightly as she instructed Layne to carry in the tacos. She wanted to race straight to the bedroom, but Layne pleaded that he needed to pass out his gift of tacos before they got there.

Layne systematically went from room to room, handing out tacos as if he were Santa with a giant bag of presents. Hungover faces turned to smiles as the food was presented. Lila helped in the gift giving, only to speed the process along. For any stragglers who may come along, Layne left a hefty pile of tacos and hot sauce on the dining room table for anyone to enjoy. Knowing that it was time to look at her pictures, Lila dragged Layne upstairs as quickly as she could. He bounced along the stairs, trying his best not to fall over as Lila pulled him, tacos still in hand. She exploded through the bedroom door, startling Stacy awake as Layne followed her in.

Layne sympathized with Stacy. "We brought you some food," he said as he showed her the offerings.

"Right on, tacos," Stacy cried out as she sat up in bed.

"Stacy, look!" Lila exclaimed as she held the envelope in front of Stacy. "I got the photos from my new camera developed," she said with pride.

Layne climbed on the bed with the girls as him and Stacy dug into the food. Lila was busy tearing open her envelope to get to the pictures. She reached in and pulled them out carefully into her hands as her excitement became real. Layne looked over to see the beautiful black and white pictures Lila had taken. He was overcome with memories from a few days before as he saw the pictures she had taken downtown on their walk. She laid the pictures of Layne across the bed for Stacy to see as well. Stacy became ecstatic as she saw the photos, and asked about the details behind the pictures. Lila was filled with enthusiasm as she told Stacy all about their morning that day.

Layne admired the pictures that he had not expected. Lila showed him the pictures she took around Thompson's house of the trees and flowers. "When did you have time to take these?" he asked.

"Yesterday," she replied. "Right after you left for your sound check, I walked around for a bit and took these shots," she said as she pointed them out to him.

"Oh yeah," he realized. "That makes sense," he added with a smile before biting into his taco.

"Which one's your favorite?" he asked with a mouth full of food.

Lila took a moment to look over the images before finally picking one out. "I think this one," she said, as she handed him the photo.

Layne studied the picture in his hand. It was the first picture she had taken of him while he was walking down the street with his guitar slung across his back.

Stacy glanced over Layne's shoulder. "That's an amazing shot Lila."

"What's your favorite?" Lila asked Layne, curious as to his opinion.

"Hmm, let me see," Layne looked over the photos carefully, not wanting to make his decision too quickly. "This one," he finally decided as he handed the photo to Lila. "The picture I took of you in the basement. Look at the way you're straddling my guitar," he pointed out. "And the way you have your hair flowing down over your right shoulder. You look absolutely beautiful," he added sincerely.

"I like that one too," Lila agreed with a kiss on Layne's cheek.

Stacy added, "You know Layne, Lila almost never lets people take pictures of her."

"Oh is that right?" Layne said as he turned toward Lila with his big-hearted smile.

"If you remember correctly, I didn't *let* you take that picture of me, you just took it," she protested. "But I really do like it," she added with a smile matching Layne's.

"You're an amazing photographer by the way," Layne praised. "I really do love all of them. I can't wait to see what else you can capture with that camera."

"I know!" she proclaimed. "I'm so excited to use it all the time now."

Lila gently gathered her photos into an organized and neat pile before carefully slipping them back into the envelope. She realized how hungry she was after they were all put away and began eating with Layne and Stacy.

Downstairs, the clean up effort was in full effect as Lila, Layne and Stacy emerged from the room. Music blasted through the house, providing an energetic backbone. Garbage bags were passed around to any and everyone as the partiers scoured the rooms. Instead of the usual monotonous task, the music transformed the cleaning ritual into a festive event. Thompson and Jeff soon followed the sounds of commotion, leading them to the happy surprise of tacos. Joe and Nicole stumbled in soon after. The Turkish room quickly became the unofficial break room as hungover patrons took breaks from cleaning the spilled beer. Cigarette smoke billowed out of the door each and every time it was left open. Shoes and miscellaneous lost articles of clothing were gathering on the dining room table. Layne and Joe joked about how some of the clothing could have possibly been left behind.

Joe carefully picked up a pink mini skirt with his thumb and index fingers. "Dude, how does some girl leave a skirt behind?" Joe asked, as he tried his best to think of a possible scenario. "Think about it. Some girl wore this skirt to the party, takes it off at some point, and then just goes home in her underwear? Not even realizing she forgot something?"

Layne laughed as he thought about the proposed situation. "I don't know man, people are weird sometimes."

Joe chuckled, "Yeah, I guess so."

Once the mess from the party was cleaned, and the house was returned to its usual disastrous state, Layne gathered Joe, Thompson and Katelyn, in order to fix the broken instruments. The rest of the group filed into the basement as the band and Katelyn began piecing the guitar and drums back together. Katelyn systematically arranged the pieces of the guitar across the table as the rest slowly glued the pieces back together.

"You really messed this one up Layne," Katelyn announced as she oversaw the project. "You'll be lucky to get through another weekend with this without it falling apart on stage."

"What?" Layne laughed as Katelyn shot him a displeased look. "I got a little excited," he pleaded.

"A little excited and destroying everything on stage are two very different things," Katelyn scowled.

The guitar went back together faster that Katelyn had thought. Joe and Thompson added the clamps to hold the glued pieces in place as Layne carefully checked the guitar's alignment. The growing audience of friends patiently waited around the operation, waiting to see how the guitar would turn out. After the last clamp was successfully set in place, the surgeons were pleased. They turned their attention to the drum set. Each piece was carefully inspected as the damage was assessed.

"The snare drum seems to be. . .destroyed," Katelyn announced as she turned the drum in her hands.

"The floor tom looks perfectly fine, it may have been pushed out of the way," Thompson added as he inspected the legs of the tom.

Joe cradled a tom in his hands. "This one needs new heads, and it looks like this support shaft is bent."

"Thompson what do you think?" Layne asked. "Heat it and bend it with a Torch or maybe just a vise?"

Lee chimed in to lend a helping hand as he appeared from his basement cave, "I can take it to work and straighten that out no problem." He then looked over the broken guitar as he grunted to himself.

The five of them discussed the best ways of fixing the drums in as little time as possible. Discussions rang out as to which music store would be the cheapest to order the broken parts, as well as which items Lee would take to work with him.

As the rest of the damage was dealt with, Jeff turned to Lila, "So." He began to ask, "After all of this, how was your weekend?"

"Amazing!" she replied with a giant smile across her face. "It has to be the best weekend I've ever had! There was so much fun and excitement the entire time, and I'm so glad I got to meet all of you!" Lila boosted as she glowed with happiness.

Jeff stirred his mimosa as he watched Lila's expressions. "I'm so happy to hear that. You're welcome back anytime, we really do love having you around."

"Thank you Jeff," she said kindly. "I guess now I'll definitely have to come back, especially since my boyfriend is going to be living here in a few weeks," she added with wink.

"Boyfriend!" Jeff nearly shouted as he took a sip of his drink to calm down. "Oh my goodness! This is so exciting, when did this happen?"

Lila laughed as Stacy interrupted, "Yeah! When did this happen?"

"This morning actually," Lila responded with pride as she glanced towards Layne across the room.

Stacy was shocked. "Isn't that moving a little fast?"

Jeff took another sip of his drink. "I saw the way you two look at each other, sometimes love has a way of working rather quickly, and there's nothing wrong with that," he added with a wink. "I really do think this could be something special. It's about time someone made him happy. I've already seen a new glow in his eyes just in the past few days."

Layne gathered his guitars after the instruments were inspected. Lila offered to help as she strung one over her shoulder and grabbed another in her open hand. Layne instructed that he planned to leave them in the bedroom instead of driving them across town to his parent's house. She followed him with the guitars back to the bedroom where he carefully displayed them along the wall. Lila folded the blankets that were used the night before as Layne returned the futon into a couch. After the room was in order, Lila took a seat on the couch alongside Layne as he pulled one of his guitars across his lap and began strumming a soft melody.

"I love it when you play for me," she said lovingly.

"I'm sure you'll grow sick of it after hearing me play all the time," he joked as he picked the strings.

"I don't see how I could ever grow tired of it," she replied with her smile.

Layne strummed the guitar and began singing softly to Lila. She was captivated by his world and never wanted to leave. She curled her body close to his as she gently placed her head on his shoulder. His deep voice reverberated through her body, warming her soul. For the first time, in as long as she could remember, she was completely at peace in the moment. Lila closed her eyes as he sang, hanging on to every emotion he portrayed as it came alive in the room. She gently began to sing along in harmony with him. Notes and melodies danced around in her head as the music flowed through her body. She knew that he would be leaving soon and she tried her best to hang on as long as she could.

As the song came to an end, Layne let the last note ring out of the guitar as long as he could before it fell silent in the room. He felt it as well, and knew that he did not want to leave. He was afraid of losing this perfect girl he had just gotten to know.

"Lila, I need to get going. I have to catch the 3:10 back to Fresno," he said softly.

"Are you sure you have to go now? You can't stay a little longer?" she questioned anxiously.

"I wish I could, but I still have a bit of homework I need to finish before class tomorrow. I didn't get it all done Friday night," he said desperately. "And I wasn't planning on coming home next weekend because I have finals to study for, but maybe I could try to come see you."

Lila looked up into his big blue eyes. "If you get time, I would love to see you next weekend," she said with her warm smile. "But only if you have free time, finals are more important right now, and I'll see you as soon as I can, I promise."

He leaned over and kissed her without saying a word.

Layne finally got up from the couch and grabbed the guitar bag with his precious red guitar inside, before leading Lila out of the room.

The dining room was full of all of his friends, waiting for Layne to say goodbye. Lila watched from the doorway as he hugged each and every one of them. She admired how close of a group they all were. His friends were like his family and the bonds between them were incredibly strong. Katelyn forced Lila to join while she greeted her with a warm hug. Stacy joined in as well, with Timothy telling her how wonderful it was to meet her. Stacy and Lila realized quickly that they had been fully accepted.

Lila decided to ride with Layne to the train station to say her goodbye there. She was not quite ready to let him go. Stacy agreed to follow them in her car, as the vehicles sped off down the road, leaving the friends in a long line across the sidewalk.

CHAPTER 14

Lila gripped onto Layne's hand as he shifted through the gears. He could feel her unsettling emotions as he drove through the streets. He tried to think of any way to ease her stress, but the words fell short. A song on the radio had been playing in the background that neither of them were listening too. After the song ended, Bob Marley came on the radio with Three Little Birds as Lila turned the volume up. Layne smiled and sang along as Lila joined in. The smooth melodies and vibes of the song calmed them both down, as they realized there was nothing to worry about. Layne drummed along on the steering wheel as he listened to Lila sing, admiring her voice. Feeling confident, she projected her voice louder to match his as they harmonized.

Stacy pulled into the train station parking lot and parked beside the mustang. Layne and Lila were already grabbing Lila's bags from the trunk as her car came to a rest. She quickly opened the trunk so the luggage could be transferred smoothly.

"Is that everything?" Layne asked Lila.

"Yeah. I don't think I'm forgetting anything," she replied as she looked over her bags.

Layne's train slowly pulled into the station as he gently put the strap of the guitar case over his shoulder. Lila looked up from her bags to see the boy of her dreams standing before her. His mirrored aviator sunglasses, the blue flannel jacket, and the guitar across his back accented his personality perfectly as it clung tight.

Layne studied Lila, never wanting to forget any moment or detail about her. Her long dark hair glowed beautifully in the afternoon sunlight. She had her mirrored sunglasses carefully protecting her eyes from the stray beams of light. Lila still wore Layne's flannel, which he did not mind at all. It seemed to fit her personality perfectly.

He carefully removed his sunglasses as he walked towards her. She saw his advances and did the same. Once again, they were locked in a loving embrace, staring deep into each other's eyes. The tension built until she could no longer take it. Pressing her feet down to lift her body closer to his, she kissed him as he wrapped his arms tight around her. This time, no music had to play in their heads, alluding to a fantasy world, this was real and they felt it.

"I have something for you," Lila said in a soft whisper as she slowly pulled away from him.

She reached into the envelope with her pictures inside, and pulled out the picture he had taken of her. She studied the photograph for a moment before handing it over to Layne. He instantly filled with happiness as he looked down at the picture.

"I love this one," he mustered with a smile.

"I know you do," she replied, equally as happy. "I can put it in the pocket of your guitar bag if you would like."

"That would be perfect!" he exclaimed as he handed her the picture.

"There," she said after she closed the bag. "Now you can keep a piece of me with you," she added with a smile.

He kissed her again before turning towards Stacy to give her a hug. They each quickly said goodbye before Layne walked towards the train by himself. Lila and Stacy watched in silence as he boarded the train and disappeared without ever turning back.

CHAPTER 15

Layne gazed out the window as the train rolled through the country. He assumed they must have been nearing Madera soon. After all of his train rides, he had gotten to know every inch of the country as the train steamed along. Feeling every bump and bend in the tracks, he related to the train on an emotional level. Layne imagined that the train was his vessel through life, elegantly guiding him to his next destination. This past weekend, he thought, threw a curve ball in his vision. He felt as if the train had stopped mid tracks just long enough for him to take a look around and admire the beauty of the world just for a moment. He tried his best to comprehend what Lila's role could be in all of this. His smile grew bigger across his face as he imagined the perfect life with her in it.

He carefully inspected the guitar bag in the seat next to him, knowing how special the contents were. The music in his ears pulsed through the headphones as he replayed the weekend over and over in his mind. He could not help to shake the smile he had plastered across his face throughout the entire ride. As his phone vibrated, he glanced down at a text from Lila. He thought about calling her before he went to bed, just so that he could hear her voice. Picking up the phone from his lap, he quickly responded to her message and began flipping through his music library to pick out the next song. The ideas rushed through his head as he imagined his life with Lila.

He had left her less than two hours before and already could not wait to be back in her arms again.

Something caught his eye as he stopped on a song. Layne quickly looked out the window to see a beautiful red airplane flying low through the fields as it glistened in the afternoon sun. As the song played through his headphones, he marveled at the elegance of the plane's movements, before realizing he was listening to Jack Johnson's "Breakdown". He imagined what it would feel like to fly and feel so free. He watched attentively as the plane sprayed the fields no more than ten feet from the ground before flying under the live power lines that stretched across the horizon. The adrenaline rush must be amazing, he thought to himself. He wondered if he would ever get to experience a feeling of that magnitude before realizing that he already does. It may be like the feeling he had when he was on stage, the thought drifted through his mind.

He had been unhappy for so long that at times he had forgotten what it felt like. In his own weird way, he projected what he felt happiness should be onto everyone else, and by making other people happy, in turn, it made him happy. Maybe that's the reason for playing music, the channels of thought finally concluded.

He once again wondered who the man was and what his story may be. Maybe his life would read like a good book. Maybe he would be a wonderful storyteller with a raspy voice filled with suspense and awe. He would probably never know how lucky he is, Layne thought to himself. That guy must be the happiest man in the world. Watching intently as the plane rose above the clouds before diving down into the fields, he could not help but think he did not pick the song; the song picked him.

ABOUT THE AUTHOR

Christopher Barry was born and lives in the California Central Valley city of Stockton. He has enjoyed writing stories from a young age. His hobbies include playing guitar and writing music. He loves the outdoors jet skiing and boating on the Delta, hiking in the mountains, biking in the city and along the country roads, and free diving in the Pacific Ocean.

Made in the USA
Coppell, TX
27 July 2020